COMPLETELY CASSIDY

ACCIDENTAL GENIUS

For the pupils of Oakmere Primary School and
The Wroxham School, who know READING TOTALLY ROCKS.

First published in 2015 by Usborne Publishing Ltd.,
Usborne House, 83-85 Saffron Hill, London EC1N 8RT, England.
www.usborne.com

Cover and inside illustrations by Antonia Miller.
Title lettering by Stephen Raw.

A CIP catalogue record for this book is available from the British Library.

JFM MJJASOND/15

ISBN 9781409562719 02954/3

Printed in Chatham, Kent, UK.

COMPLETELY CASSIDY

ACCIDENTAL GENIUS

TAMSYN MURRAY

USBORNE

CHAPTER ONE

My life is a joke. Actually, that's not true – it's too
TRAGIC to be funny – but it IS a total disaster. You
might think that I sound a teensy bit DRAMA-QUEEN-ISH
here but that's only because you don't know the full horror.
You see, tomorrow is my first day at secondary school and
already I know I am going to be the girl everyone points
at, laughing. Honestly, it will be worse than the time I
accidentally flashed my bobbly grey pants in assembly
when I was five and earned the nickname MISS NAPPY
KNICKERS for a whole year, and that was bad enough.

For a start, I have the most ridiculous name in the history of names – I mean, who calls their baby girl CASSIDY? My parents, that's who, although it's not as bad as MOON UNIT, which is what some old rock star called his daughter. Parents should have to submit their name choices to some kind of baby-name court before they are allowed to put them on the birth certificate. It would save a lot of teasing later on. Still, it's all very well starting primary school with a weird name – everyone is too busy with the play-dough to take much interest – but secondary school is different. I don't want to think about how many sniggers there'll be when the very first register is called.

I'd probably be able to cope if that was the end of THE NIGHTMARE; it isn't. Even worse than having the world's stupidest name is the disgusting school blazer I am expected to wear. Seriously, it's so ENORMOUS that my fingertips are barely visible at the end of the sleeves and the shoulders look like something the eighties threw out. In fact, it used to fit my brother, Liam, and since he is a fourteen-year-old GIGANTOR and I am eleven, this is a total disaster. There is a big hole in the lining of the inside pocket which is just waiting for me to lose things through. And then there's the smell of mouldy old grass and stinky feet.

I SUPPOSE I should be grateful that it doesn't stink as badly as Liam does but silver linings are hard to find when you smell like THE GIRL THAT DEODORANT FORGOT.

Mum doesn't seem to care. I've been telling her for weeks that I needed a new uniform but she didn't listen to me. Honestly, it's like I'm not even there sometimes. So of course we didn't go to the uniform shop until the last weekend of the holidays and they had no small blazers left. And still Mum didn't seem bothered, not even when she saw Liam laughing and my bottom lip wobbling – she just rubbed her MASSIVE BABY BUMP in a tired way and said, "Stop blubbing, Cassie. It won't kill you to wear Liam's old one for a few days."

There wasn't much I could say to that – technically she is right. I'm not likely to die from wearing Liam's cast-offs (although there is a suspiciously gloopy substance in one pocket that looks like it could be a BIOHAZARD) but it's not going to win me any coolness points either. In fact, she might as well have tattooed a gigantic L on my forehead. It's at times like these I wish I was an orphan – not Oliver Twist, obviously. A rich one and preferably royal.

Anyway, you see my problem? I tried texting Molly and Shenice for advice but they were worse than useless. Molly suggested folding the sleeves back like she saw in last month's GLITZ magazine. I told her it might work with a sassy little on-trend blazer but a one hundred per cent polyester IRON-EZE special was more resistant to fashion adjustments. Shenice replied that there were kids in Africa without any clothes who would love to have my blazer problems. Maybe I can offer to donate it to COMIC RELIEF. They could probably use it as a tent.

I know exactly what you're going to say – why don't I tell my mum I have developed a HORRIFICALLY CONTAGIOUS disease and thus avoid school? Well, I was thinking of that, too, when I bumped into Liam on the landing. He looked me up and down and sniggered.

"The Incredible Hulk called. He wants his blazer back."

Then he went into his room, smirking like he was Windsor's answer to Michael McIntyre, and completely missing the fact that he'd just insulted himself. He is such a moron. I'm sure you totally see why I hate him – even the Dalai Lama would find it hard to like him and it's his job to love everyone. Shenice's half-brother is seventeen and he brings her loads of cool stuff when he comes round, plus he lets her listen to PARENTAL ADVISORY songs. All Liam does is make stupid jokes about me and moans when Mum and Dad make him babysit. If he thinks I'm a pain to have around, he should wait until the twins arrive. Molly said she saw her little cousin wee into his dad's face when he was a baby, so I am really hoping the twins will be on my side in THE WAR OF THE SIBLINGS.

By the time I'd stopped pulling faces at his closed door and gone downstairs, Mum had just finished stitching my name into the rest of my new uniform. She didn't buy the illness thing.

"Cassidy Bond, you do not have malaria," she snapped when I reeled off the symptoms I'd looked up online. "And stop going on about your blazer. It doesn't smell that bad. Roll the sleeves up if they're too long."

It's alright for her, she's six months pregnant — NOTHING is too big for her. But she looked quite cross when I pointed that out so I decided not to mention that the badge is sewn on wonky as well. Pregnant women seem to be very grumpy — or maybe it is just my mum.

So now I am lying in bed, wishing it was always Saturday night and never Sunday and trying to think of another way to avoid school tomorrow. Maybe if I wish hard enough, a freak blizzard will appear out of nowhere, causing everyone to be snowed in and the school to be closed. That would be pretty cool. Who knows, I might have an undiscovered talent for controlling the weather — I've never actually tried it. Maybe I am secretly a MUTANT, like the ones in the X-MEN movies. I wouldn't mind so much if I was — I bet Wolverine never had to wear a badly fitting school uniform.

What my mum doesn't seem to get is that I am REALLY worried about tomorrow and not just because of the **THING THAT CANNOT BE NAMED** (currently in a heap on my bedroom floor). I mean, I knew where I was at Westwood Primary – me, Shenice and Molly were BFFs from day one and, between us, we knew everyone.

St Jude's is much bigger and will be full of fun-poking strangers (apart from Liam and his stupid mates, who are so horrible that I wish I **DIDN'T** know them). What if I get lost? What if I look at one of the Year Tens funny and they thump me? What if I get so much homework that I don't have time for my besties? Although now I come to think of it, Liam never seems to have that much homework but that's because he reckons he's going to be a rock star (ha ha) and doesn't care about school. Dad said last week that Liam has to **BUCK HIS IDEAS UP** this year or his guitar will be confiscated. This can only be a good thing as far as I am concerned. It sounds like he is strangling next door's cat when he plays it.

Molly and Shenice are worried, too, even though they are pretending not to be. We are putting what my dad calls "a brave face" on it and talking as though it will be the BEST THING EVER. I doubt we will survive the first day. In some ways, I hope I am vaporized by the scornful look of a passing Year Eleven. Then my parents will be sorry they made me wear THE BLAZER OF STINKY BIGFOOT. Oh yes, they will.

Page torn out of Mum's book
THE UNIVERSAL ORDERING SERVICE ↘

Getting what you want out of life

The secret to getting what you want out of life is simple – ask the universe to give it to you! You want a new lipgloss, new look, new life? All you need to do is say it out loud and the universe will find a way to deliver.

Write down your shopping list for the universe here:

Dear Universe,

What I want most is a talent – something I am really good at. Molly is a BRILLIANT singer, Shenice is the JUNIOR BERKSHIRE SWIMMING CHAMPION and Liam has his GUITAR SKILLS (such as they are). Is it too much to ask to find the thing I'm best at?

   Also, LEGS LIKE A SUPERMODEL and HAIR LIKE THE GIRL ON THE SHAMPOO advert.

Thanks!

CHAPTER TWO

I suppose I must have fallen asleep eventually because when I woke up, it was DD-DAY (which stands for DOOM AND DESPERATION DAY) and absolutely zero snowflakes had fallen while I slept. So much for the X-MEN theory. In fact, DD-DAY started exactly the way I'd expect the worst day of my life to start – with the gut-wrenching discovery that Rolo had eaten one of my brand-new school shoes. I mean, how typical is that? The first time I manage to persuade Mum to buy me a decent pair and my stupid dog has destroyed them.

"You shouldn't have left them lying around," Mum sniffed, when I showed her the gnawed remains of a patent leather ballet pump. "I told you when you asked for a puppy that Labradors like to chew things. Now you'll have to wear the old ones. Or those sensible lace-ups Auntie Jane bought you."

She said it like it is somehow my fault that we have a dog who eats everything from socks to soap bars. I mean, I admit he is my dog – we got him for my tenth birthday, back before we knew Mum and Dad were about to DOUBLE the number of mouths they had to feed. Back then I had this vague idea that Labradors played with toilet rolls all day and helped blind people cross the road.

ROLO was the only chocolate puppy in a litter of wishy-washy yellow ones and leaped enthusiastically all over his brothers and sisters to get to us. It wasn't until we got him home and he taste-tested next door's tabby that we realized we might have made a mistake. By then it was too late.

My old shoes are navy blue leather, with kittens embroidered on the front and I don't mean in a retro HELLO KITTY way either. And the lace-ups from Auntie Jane make me feel about eighty. In other words, they are both a complete no-no for your first day at secondary school. Of course, my mother is completely oblivious to what is acceptable to the Year Seven fashionistas. A few minutes after her last ridiculous instruction, she waddled past looking for the car keys and threw me an impatient look. "Cassidy, you cannot stick those pumps together with sticky tape. Find the kitten ones, now. You don't want to be late on your first day."

Actually, I did. About seven hours late would have suited me fine but she pretended to have gone deaf when

I said so. Liam was typically unsympathetic. He snorted when he saw my feet on the way to the car.

"If anyone asks, tell them you're adopted, okay? I've got a rep to protect at ST CRUDE'S."

I thought about telling him that I wish I WAS adopted but Mum was listening and she gets upset when I say that. For someone who claims to love me, she doesn't seem to show it. If she really cared, she'd let me stay at home today.

And for the next seven years.

So, as you've probably guessed, Mum made me go. She went all misty-eyed when we got to the school gates, insisting on hugging AND kissing me goodbye — I think she'd have come into the actual playground if I'd let her. It's a good thing the twins are on their way; maybe when she has real babies to look after, she'll stop treating me like one. Things didn't improve when we got to registration. I thought I'd die of shame as I gazed around at the pristine blazers of my new classmates and wondered if they'd noticed my slightly frayed lapel and **AROMA OF TEENAGE BOY**. I wouldn't blame them for laughing behind my back – combined with the kittens, I wasn't exactly looking my best. But no one said anything nasty, not even when the register was called, although I'm grateful to **JUSTIN TYME** for taking most of the heat there. It helped that Shen and Molly and me seem to be in all the same classes, at least for now – they distracted me from my wardrobe disasters with a stream of silly comments and jokes. Honestly, they should have their own TV show or something – they are SO funny.

After registration, we moved rooms to English (**YAY!**) and maths (**NOT SO YAY**) and between my hilarious BFFs and the friendly teachers, I was amazed to realize our first morning was actually fun. I even managed to forget Liam's existence until the beginning of lunchtime. We were in the queue for the canteen when I felt something block out the sun and looked up to see him looming over me.

"Alright, dweeb?" he said, and his idiot mates all sniggered like it was the funniest thing ever. "Embarrassed yourself yet?"

"Do I know you?" I asked.

He reached out and rubbed hard at my hair with his bony fist, the way he knows I hate. "Give us some of your dinner money."

"Where's yours?" I said, ducking out of reach with a scowl.

"I lost it."

Huh, spent it on sweets more like. But his mates were all staring at me

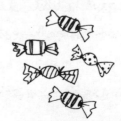

20

like I had six heads and it was making me uncomfortable. I wanted them to go away and there was only one sure-fire way to achieve that. Sticking my hand inside the safe pocket, not the RADIOACTIVE one, I pulled out my Minnie Mouse purse. "Mum won't be happy about this."

He took the money I held out and smiled. "Which is why you're not going to tell her about it. Laters, dweeb."

"It must be nice to have a big brother like Liam," Molly said when he'd gone, staring after him with a weirdly wistful look on her face.

"Oh yeah, it's BRILLIANT," I replied, injecting the words with as much withering sarcasm as I could manage. "I especially love it when he leaves me with hardly any money to feed myself for the day."

She let out a sigh. "But he totally cherishes you as his

little sister, right? He'd be there for you when it mattered?"

Shenice and I exchanged looks. Molly is an only child in an otherwise big Greek family and she has strange ideas about what having siblings is really like — I'm sure she thinks we go off and have secret FAMOUS FIVE adventures when she's not looking. She's not allowed pets, either, so she goes nuts over Rolo. Folding my arms, I pretended to think about the question.

"Let's see. If I was the one without any money, do you think he'd share what he had with me?"

She began to nod. I cut her off with a pitying look. "No, he would not."

A soppy smile crossed her face. "He's got great hair, though. And a cute smile."

My jaw all but smashed into the concrete at our feet — when had she ever seen Liam smiling? He hardly comes out of his room when my friends are round and wears a permanent sneer if he does. "Molly Papadopoulos, you are not thinking what I think you're thinking?"

Molly looked guilty. "What? I'm just saying he's not a bad-looking boy. It doesn't mean I want to get married or anything."

"Sounds to me like you fancy him," Shenice said in a sing-song voice. "Molly lo-oves Liam!"

"I don't!" Molly squeaked, turning redder than her packed lunch bag. "As if anyone would fancy Cassidy's smelly brother, anyway. I'd rather snog Mr Brundell. Yuck, yuck, yuckitty yuck."

Mr Brundell was the ancient caretaker at our old school. I don't know what was worse, Shenice's off-key singing or Molly's attraction to an OAP. Besides, it seemed like she was protesting a bit too much. NO ONE wants to kiss Mr Brundell, not even my mum, and they are practically the same age. Molly must have realized I was a bit freaked out, though. She didn't say anything but she did buy me a Wham bar on the way home, which is the universal peace offering between the three of us. But it'll take a lot more than a sugary bribe to make me forget her soppiness, I can tell you that.

Still, at least that was the worst thing to happen all day. And nobody picked on me, which was a definite plus. Tomorrow might be another matter entirely, which is a deeply depressing thought. Am I really expected to endure seven whole years of the same TORTURE? It's inhuman. There should be a law against it. In fact, I might write to the Prime Minister right now. In Victorian times, children didn't have to go to school, they were allowed to get a job instead. I'm not saying I want to be a chimney sweep (although have you seen MARY POPPINS? It looks like fun) but it would be nice to have the option. Surely making important decisions like that is what being Prime Minister is all about?

Things took a nosedive when I got home. Mum had left my bedroom door open when she'd been getting my washing and Rolo must have followed her because there were muddy paw prints and blobs of grass-filled puke all over my duvet cover. It just about sums my life up. Seriously, Hagrid, when are you getting here with my invitation to Hogwarts? WHEN????

Sometimes it helps you to be **more positive** if you count your blessings.

Use this space to write down a few things you like about the life you're living now:

* My eyes – they are grey with gold bits in the middle, like my dad's, with really long eyelashes. Thankfully, I didn't also get his hair, which is all wiry like one of those saucepan-scrubbing things. Although given the choice, I wouldn't have gone for mousy brown either. Thanks, genetics.

* I can lick my own elbow. Apparently, it's not that rare but I've never met anyone else who can do it. Until the universe gets busy with my order, it is my only talent.

* My BFFs – Molly and Shenice are both ace. I am really lucky to have them.

...continued
(clearly stuff is not as bad as I thought)

* My parents are still together. Shenice's mum
  and dad split up when we were in Year Three
  and her dad has this horrible girlfriend who is
  much younger than him. I hope Mum and Dad
  never get divorced.

* I am not ugly. Okay, I'm not a supermodel,
  either, but I am what my nan calls
  "presentable". I might wish for Molly's curls or
  Shenice's creamy light-brown skin but I don't
  mind looking like me.

* Rolo – he may be the world's most mental
  dog but he's MY mental dog. I wish he didn't
  always eat first and ask questions later,
  though. And maybe sometimes he could puke on
  someone else's bed?

CHAPTER THREE

I'm not one hundred per cent sure that I'm not still asleep
and dreaming this but I THINK I might
have survived the first week of St Crude's without
any major disasters. True, there was one slightly
embarrassing moment when I tripped up in front of a big
group of Year Nine boys and they chanted "She fell over!"
until we were out of earshot but since that's the kind of
thing that happens to me all the time, it hardly counts.
Even more astonishingly, Mum seemed to notice that
I've been STRESSY MCSTRESSED and asked if I wanted

a sleepover with Molly and Shenice on Friday night. This never happens, unless it is my birthday, because of an unfortunate incident a few years ago involving Mum's straighteners and Molly's ringlets. I don't know why everyone got so upset – they grew back eventually, although the straighteners never quite lost the singed smell.

Mum also offered to give me some money to go shoe shopping on Saturday morning. I guess it is the pregnancy hormones making her act WEIRZOID but I half-wondered if my real mother had been abducted and replaced by a nice-seeming alien who would experiment on us while we slept. Until I saw her dipping CHEESE STRINGS into a pot of apricot jam, that was. What is it with pregnancy and disgusting food combos, anyway? I'm telling you, the more I see, the more certain I become that I am NEVER having children.

Anyway, Shenice and Molly and me were sitting on my

bed in our pyjamas, munching a packet of
Oreo cookies and trying to ignore the
tortured sound of Liam's guitar
screeching through the wall. Shenice
had just asked whether I'd be mates
with, date or slate the lead singer
from THE DROIDS.

"Duh," I said, pointing at the poster on my wall. "Have
you seen him? Date, obviously."

"Okay, you can have Rory," Shenice said generously.
"As long as I get Ziggy. Molly, which one do you want?"

Molly sniffed. "I prefer real musicians. Ones who can
actually play their instruments instead of pretending to.
The Droids are a manufactured band – they don't deserve
to be successful."

A particularly loud wail pierced the air. I frowned;

unlike my brother, she'd certainly changed her tune. "You sound like Liam. That's the kind of thing he comes out with every Saturday night."

She went a bit pink. "He's right. And I bet his band is much better. What are they called again?"

My frown deepened. It wasn't at all like Molly not to join in with our endless conversations about Rory and Ziggy and Joel. Where had all this rubbish about real musicians come from? I shook my head, confused. "Something stupid like **DOG BREATH**. And no, they're not better than The Droids. They can't sing, for a start. They kind of shout the words instead, like they're angry about everything."

"At least The Droids boys are cute," Shenice put in, staring at my poster with a longing sigh. "Liam and his band mates look like a bunch of fourteen-year-olds trying to be cool."

Probably because they ARE a bunch of fourteen-year-olds trying to be cool.

"Yeah, wait until you see Liam tomorrow, when he's just dragged himself out of his pit and his hair is waxed to his nose," I said, my voice heavy with scorn. "You won't think he's so ace then."

Molly stuck out her chin in a way I knew meant she was up for a fight. I'd seen that look plenty, like when she launched herself at Jake Marshall in Year Three for stealing her TAMAGOTCHI and her mum got called in to see the Headteacher. Shenice must have recognized the warning signs too, because she hurriedly picked up the Oreos packet and shook it. "We're out of supplies. Got anything else to eat, Cass?"

"Let's go and raid the fridge," I suggested, grateful for the diversion. "Mum's got a family bag of Maltesers in there — one of you can create a distraction and I'll smuggle them upstairs while she's not looking."

For once, I was actually glad to bump into Liam on the landing. He was bound to ignore us completely and Molly would see how horrible he was. But she had other plans.

"Hi, Liam," she said, smiling at him.

I waited for the inevitable snub.

"Oh, hi, ladies," he replied, flicking his heavyweight fringe out of his eyes. "How you doing?"

I rolled my eyes. If there's one thing Liam isn't, it's smooth enough to pull off a cheesy chat-up line.

But Molly was lapping it up. In fact, I swear she FLUTTERED HER EYELASHES at him. "I'm good, thanks. Loved your guitar playing, by the way."

Shenice's mouth dropped open at the exact second mine did. No one in their right mind would describe what Liam had been doing as guitar "playing". GUITAR TORTURE was more like it.

Liam grinned. "Always good to meet a fan. Molly, isn't it?"

I thought I might actually pass out. It's as much as he can do to remember my name most of the time, let alone what my mates are called.

Beaming, Molly twisted her hands in her SpongeBob pyjamas. "Yeah. I bet you're the best one in Dog Breath."

Liam's smile slipped a bit. "It's WOLF BRETHREN, actually. As in pack brothers who hear the call of the wild."

Shenice dissolved into giggles and I was

trying so hard to swallow a burst of laughter that I almost choked. Molly looked devastated, though.

"Sorry – I thought—" She broke off her apology to glare at me. "Cassie told me you were called Dog Breath. She's SO immature." And she flounced into my room, slamming the door after herself.

"Cassidy!" my dad bellowed from the living room. "Stop banging about up there. Your mother's trying to rest!"

"Yeah, Cassidy, stop banging about," Liam sneered, pulling a stupid face. "You're so immature."

"At least I don't still SUCK MY THUMB!" I fired back, and dodged the thump he threw my way. His hand thudded into the banister and he let out a whimper of pain.

"You'll pay for that," he growled, cradling his fist like

it was about to fall off. "If I miss one minute of a WOLF BRETHREN rehearsal because of you, the lads will rip you apart with their bare teeth."

He spun about and stamped into his room. The door rattled in its frame as he slammed it shut.

"Cassidy!" my dad yelled, sounding furious. "Don't make me come up there!"

I opened my mouth to shout that it wasn't even me but realized there was no point. Shenice threw me a sympathetic look and I shook my head in pity. Where was Molly when Liam showed his true colours, eh? Where?

Sighing at the injustice of it all, I squared my shoulders. "Come on, Soldier," I said to Shenice, heading for the stairs. "OPERATION: FRIDGE RAID is go."

I only hoped Mum hadn't guzzled the emergency

Maltesers in another of her baby-fuelled binges. Because if I knew anything about Molly's moods, it was that they tended to be the wrong side of epic. Without chocolate to sustain us, Shenice and I might not survive the night. As I reached into the fridge and slid out the unopened family-sized bag, I remembered the scowl on Molly's face as she'd stormed off. And although even Rory from The Droids couldn't have dragged it from me, I was a little bit hurt by her "immature" dig. Was that really what she thought of me?

Gnawing my bottom lip, I looked at the chocolate packet in my hand doubtfully.

"Know what, Shen? We're going to need a bigger bag."

To: BondGirl007
From: Ask@CrazyPetVets

Hi Cassie,

Thanks for your online enquiry about your dog, Rolo. I'm really sorry to hear you've been having problems with his behaviour. Although your description of his "Operation Shock and Awe" on next door's cat does make it sound like he is "an evil mastermind plotting to take over the world, one tabby at a time", I'm inclined to think you just have a very lively dog. I do agree that it is quite unusual for a Labrador to try to leap out of a first-floor window, even in pursuit of a pigeon – they are usually a bit smarter than that. Thank goodness it was closed!

I am also pleased to say that Rolo is likely to grow out of some of his exuberance by the age of three. You don't say whether he has been neutered but this might help to prevent him from scent-marking your school bag and also with his embarrassing attraction to your Uncle Ian's leg. Sadly, I fear his cheese obsession is here to stay.

Wishing you and Rolo all the best for the future!

Emma at Crazy Pet Vets

CHAPTER FOUR

I was feeling a lot more "GLASS HALF FULL" about my second Monday morning at St Jude's by the time it rolled around. Now that the first week was under my belt, it felt like the worst bit was over. And I'd picked up a gorge new pair of ballet pumps to replace the ones Rolo had murdered. They were black and had little hearts picked out in tiny red crystals at the back. I fell in love with them the moment I saw them and had a nail-nibbling wait while the bored-looking shop assistant went to check if they had them in my size. Even Molly liked them and she turned out to be very hard to please in the aftermath of her MEGA Liam-related strop. It had taken the combined wit of Shenice and me doing our best comedy dance-off routine to get her to crack a smile on Friday night and the mood hadn't really lifted much by the time she went home on Saturday. I really hoped she'd got over it when I slid in beside her and Shenice for double English – a moody Molly is no fun at all.

I needn't have worried – the moment Mr Bearman had explained how to do the day's work and the class broke into subdued chattering, Molly beckoned me and Shenice forward, her eyes sparkling. "Have you heard the news?"

Mum had made us listen to Radio Four in the car (or RADIO SNORE, as Liam and I call it) but I didn't think the global economic crisis was the kind of news Molly meant. "About what?"

Molly looked even more gleeful. "There's a rumour

going around that the school is planning a ST JUDE'S HAS GOT TALENT competition."

"Shut up!" Shenice breathed, her brown eyes suddenly saucer-like.

I felt a thrill of excitement and immediately started to wonder who would enter and what hidden talents would be revealed. I could just picture myself wowing the entire school with my amazing talent. Of course, I'd have to work out what my talent was first, but that was a minor detail. Everyone has something they're really good at, right? "Who told you there's going to be a talent contest?"

"Nathan Crossfield's mum is on the PTA and he says it's all been agreed." Molly cleared her throat. "I'm sure Liam will be excited when he finds out. Wouldn't it be great if WOLF BRETHREN won?"

The image of me surrounded by flowers, adoring fans and a crying Simon Cowell vanished as I let out a loud snort. "That's never gonna happen, unless they hold a ST JUDE'S HAS GOT NO TALENT as well." I grinned at my own joke. Shenice cackled on cue but Molly didn't even smile and I remembered she'd had a sense of humour fail where Liam was concerned. Maybe I'd better steer clear of bad-mouthing my brother around her. "Who else do you think will enter?"

She shrugged. "Everyone, I suppose. There's another rumour that some of the teachers are going to do a MAMMA MIA medley."

"As long as it's not Elvis Presley." I shuddered. "Anything but that."

Sometimes, I wonder if my parents are having a competition to see who can embarrass me the most. My dad works in an office during the day, doing what sounds like the dullest job ever. Nothing embarrassing about that, you might think, and you'd be right. I wouldn't mind if that was his only job, but at night, he – well, there's no way I can make this sound good so I may as well just come out with it – at night, he sometimes moonlights as an ELVIS IMPERSONATOR. How toe-curlingly hideous is that? I remember waking up in the night once when I was about five and meeting him on the stairs just as he was heading out to do a gig. I'm not sure what traumatized me more, the WONKY BLACK WIG or the TERRIBLE FAKE TAN, but Mum says my screams woke the neighbours five houses away.

Shenice folded her arms. "You won't catch me showing myself up onstage. I don't mind helping you do it, though."

She winked at me and I scowled back. "Thanks, Shen," I said, giving her a dead-eyed look. "Going all out for FRIEND OF THE YEAR, I see."

Actually, I kind of got where she was coming from in my case. I'd fallen off the stage in at least two of our nativity performances over the years and the only time I'd ever been trusted with lines, I'd frozen with fear and peed my pants. In my defence, I should point out that I was only five years old at the time.

Shenice rolled her eyes. "You know what I mean. And don't try to tell me you're not thinking of entering – I can see it in your eyes."

I sniffed; she knew me too well. I noticed she didn't suggest that Molly would be showing herself up by performing. Then again, Molly sang like an ANGEL and probably stood a decent chance of winning. I didn't even need to ask if she'd be entering.

Molly leaned towards us again. "There's also going to be some sort of Year Seven INTER-SCHOOL QUIZ THING this term. Nathan says the teachers are supposed to be on the lookout for BRAINBOXES to represent St Jude's."

It wasn't in the same league as winning a talent contest but I could totally imagine myself helping St Jude's become QUIZ CHAMPIONS, too. Not that I was likely to get headhunted to join the team; I've never considered myself smart, although I like to think I could be clever, if I wanted to be.

Then something occurred to me. "Wait a minute... who's this Nathan you keep going on about?"

Shenice stared at me. "You haven't heard about Nathan yet?"

I shook my head, trying to remember if either of them had mentioned him.

She folded her arms, sighing, as though I'd failed some kind of test. "He's only the COOLEST boy in Year Seven. Seriously, I heard that some of the Year Nines were asking him for style tips this morning." Her head jerked towards the other side of the classroom. "Don't look now but he's over there."

I glanced across the room and then it happened: the clouds outside the window parted to let a single brilliant shaft of light beam down upon a TANNED, BLOND-HAIRED BOY laughing with his mates, and I knew without the tiniest doubt that he was Nathan. I can't be sure, but I think an angelic chorus might have burst into song somewhere nearby. Anyway, he looked up at exactly that moment and – cue the harps – ours eyes met. Shenice hadn't been messing about when she said he was cool; any cooler and he'd be wearing icicles. But no one had mentioned he was GORGEOUS too.

"OMG, he totally caught you looking!" Shenice squeaked. "Stop staring."

But I was like a magpie who'd caught sight of a bright shiny jewel — utterly unable to look away. Until Molly landed a hefty kick on my shin and I yelped in pain.

"Sorry," she said, sounding like she was anything but. "It's for your own good. You looked like you were about to start drooling."

"I was not," I said indignantly. Rubbing my leg, I risked another glance over at Nathan. The sun had gone behind the clouds again and he had his back to me. "How come I didn't notice him last week?"

"Been on holiday in Florida," Shenice replied, gazing at the back of his head and sighing. "He only got back this weekend."

I frowned. "Then how does Molly know so much about him already?"

Molly waved an airy hand. "Oh, me and Nathan go all the way back to playgroup, although obviously he didn't go to Westwood Primary with us. He lives a few doors down from me; we've been neighbours all our lives."

Shenice and I exchanged glances; I couldn't believe she'd kept such a HOTTIE secret from us. For YEARS. Anyone would think she was scared we would embarrass her or something equally ridiculous. I don't know what she thought we'd do; Shenice and I could be ice-cool when we needed to be. Like that time when we saw the bloke who plays Mr Tumble at the bookshop in town – we hardly squealed at all AND we got his autograph.

"Do you think he'll enter the talent contest?" I asked, imagining Nathan fronting a band or busting a move on the stage.

Molly shook her head and shot me a withering look. "Nah, he's too smart for all that. I reckon he'll get snapped up for the quiz team."

Good looks and intelligence? Nathan Crossfield seemed to be a cut above your average Year Seven boy; I bet he didn't think fart jokes were the height of comedy, either. It was a shame I had no chance of making this quiz team – it would have been the perfect way to get to know him without relying on Molly. But if I couldn't use my brains to get his attention, maybe there was another way to catch his eye. I'd just have to show him that Cassidy Bond had talent too.

Possible St Jude's Has Got Talent Talents

Things I am Good At:

* **Hula-hooping.** (Held school record for longest continuous hula-hooping in Year Two, no matter how many times Shenice claims to have beaten me. Check hoop still fits.)

* **Annoying Liam.** (Amusing but probably not much use for SJHGT comp.)

* **Collecting things.** (Would have completed my Panini World Cup sticker book if Liam hadn't kept stealing my stickers to sell at school.)

* **Making lists.** (Again, probably not the kind of talent Simon Cowell would be impressed by.)

* **Elbow licking.** (See previous.)

* Roller skating. (Okay, not brilliant yet and can't stop without the help of a wall, but am sure I will pick it up.)

* Magic. (Will need to find box of illusions Auntie Jane gave me two Christmases ago – think I rocked at the rope trick. Never got rabbit to appear from hat, though. May work better with next door's cat. DO NOT try with Rolo.)

* Performing Arts. (Cannot sing or dance; maybe a mime routine?)

* Cheerleading. (Have pom-poms, need the rest of costume. And rest of squad.)

* Snake charmer. (Can almost play "London's Burning" on the recorder but scared of snakes. Maybe replace snake with hamster.)

CHAPTER FIVE

Nice of the teachers at St Crude's to hit us with a trip to TEST HELL on Tuesday afternoon. Okay, so they weren't the kind of tests you can really revise for, more like those "milk is to cream as water is to—?" type questions, which I've never really got, but still — a bit of advance warning, people. It said at the top of the test sheet that they were called CATs, which made things even worse. I am definitely more of a dog person.

I nearly sat in the wrong seat as there's another girl

called C BOND in Year Seven – what are the chances of that? I don't think we're related, though, that would be too weird. Once I was in the right seat, I spent the first fifteen minutes of the test trying to see what she looked like, in case we were actually twins tragically separated at birth, until a teacher tapped me on the shoulder and told me to get on with it. I tried to answer the ridiculous questions but I admit I guessed at a few, which I suppose means I will be in the bottom set for everything. A week ago, I wouldn't have minded so much but now I want to impress Nathan and I can hardly do that if we are separated by the gulf of academic failure, can I?

It will also mean I'll be split up from Molly and Shenice for the first time since our school days began. Molly's parents thought about sending her to a private school for a while, so she had a tutor for a few months and can do these stupid tests in her sleep. Even Shenice said she didn't know what I was making such a big deal out of it for, which probably means she is an undiscovered SMARTY-PANTS and will join Molly in the top set.

The only upside of the whole sorry situation was that I got to sit at the desk across the aisle from Nathan and he smiled at me when I dropped my pen and it rolled under his chair. I'm not saying it means he'll invite me to the prom or anything but at least he knows I exist, right? I just wish it hadn't been my Tweenies pen, that's all.

So I was trying to forget about my impending academic ruin. It was proving harder than it sounded as Liam mentioned school every five minutes at dinner that night. I've never seen him so excited about St Crude's — he was in serious danger of sounding enthusiastic as he went on and on to Mum and Dad about ST JUDE'S HAS GOT TALENT.

"The winner gets two hundred and fifty quid, which me and the boys could put towards some new equipment," he said, barely pausing to shovel in some spaghetti Bolognese. "And there's a rumour that some MUSIC INDUSTRY INSIDERS will be there."

I snorted into my grated Parmesan. Even I knew that no self-respecting record label would send someone along to watch a kids' talent show in a CRUMMY old school.

Liam glared at me. "Joe Fisher's dad works for Sony, actually, and he says he's coming."

What as, I wondered, a janitor? But I didn't say it out loud.

Dad nodded. "Have you decided what you're going to play?"

For the first time, Liam's enthusiasm dipped and I knew why. Whenever anyone gets into a conversation about music with Dad, it inevitably ends up on Elvis.

Our Uncle Ian refuses to spend Christmas with us because of it. Well, that and the unfortunate time Auntie Jane and Mum got really drunk and played Knock Down Ginger on every door in our road.

"'DEATH TO THE RUNT', maybe," Liam mumbled. "Or 'BLOODLUST'."

Dad frowned. "Original material? That's risky. You'd be much better off with a cover version. I've always said you can't go wrong with a bit of 'JAILHOUSE ROCK'."

Even Mum couldn't mask a tiny heartfelt groan. Sniggering, I pictured Liam and his mates as a bunch of white-suited Elvis lookalikes. As though he could read my mind, he threw me a filthy look. "At least I've got enough talent to enter. All you're good at is showing yourself up."

"That's enough, Liam," Mum snapped. "Cassie has every right to enter the contest if she wants to." Her anxious gaze rested on me. "You're not planning on tap dancing, are you?"

I assume this was a below-the-belt reference to my short career at Twinkle Toes Tap School two summers ago, where it quickly became apparent that I had more left feet than I knew what to do with. Summoning up a mysterious smile, I waved a hand. "Don't worry, I'm not going to be dancing." Dad opened his mouth to speak but I was too quick for him. "And no, Dad, it doesn't involve Elvis."

Whatever I decide to do, it has to have the **WOW FACTOR** or Nathan will never notice me. I wonder if you can learn the trapeze from the internet?

Torn from
Glitz magazine

FIVE SIGNS HE'S THE ONE

♥ <u>You think he's gorgeous.</u>

♥ <u>He makes you laugh.</u>

♥ <u>Your friends like him.</u>

♥ <u>He likes the real you.</u>

♥ <u>He's your friend.</u>

Duh, EVERYONE thinks Nathan is gorgeous...

Not so far but we haven't actually spoken yet. He totally looks like he could.

Molly has known him since she was a toddler and says he is great — case dismissed.

Working on it, okay?

Hmm, there is no way I am telling him I sometimes still play with my Baby Annabel doll. A girl has to have some secrets.

CHAPTER SIX

Another week, another MONDAY, but this one is looking anything but good — Mum and Dad have been called into an early morning meeting with the head of Year Seven and I have to go too. I guess it is to talk about my abysmal test results. Blimey, how bad can they be? Maybe I am beyond the reach of normal school and need really serious help.

Mr Archer seemed a bit more FLUSTERED than usual as he ushered us into his tiny office, although that may have been because Mum nearly knocked him over with her baby bump. He grabbed at the desk and made a rubbish joke about assault by future pupils. I didn't smile. Would you, if you were about to be kicked out of school for being too stupid?

"Thanks for agreeing to come in and see me," Mr Archer said, sounding a bit on the cheerful side for someone who was about to chuck my entire future into a supermassive black hole. He nodded at my mum. "I appreciate it can't be easy in your – uh – condition."

Mum's face darkened the way it does when anyone hints that being pregnant is some kind of illness. Any minute now she'd launch into her **"SACRED VESSEL"** speech and my education would be over for sure. Luckily, Dad saw her expression too and got in first.

"Is Cassie in some kind of trouble?" he asked Mr Archer. I pinned my gaze to the ground. Both of my parents had asked if I knew what the meeting was about and I'd played dumb – something that I couldn't help noticing came all too easily to me. Now there was no escaping the moment of truth; they were about to discover that one of their children was an academic dud and it wasn't the one they might have suspected. Was it too much to hope for a MERCIFUL LIGHTNING STRIKE before Mr Archer frog-marched me off the premises and my humiliation became complete?

The teacher's greying eyebrows shot up at my dad's question. "Goodness me, no, quite the opposite. Cassidy here has taken us all by surprise. In fact, we think she might be one of the BRIGHTEST STUDENTS we've ever had."

I stared at him, wondering if I'd heard right. Me, bright? What in the name of LOLLIPOPS had given him that idea?

Dad was clearly wondering the same thing. He eyed me in some confusion and cleared his throat. "Really? What – uh – makes you say that?"

Mr Archer perched a pair of glasses on his nose and lifted a sheet of paper from his desk. "As you may know, we test all of our Year Seven students when they start with us, to get an idea of how they might perform. The tests are called CATs, or COGNITIVE ABILITY TESTS."

Which went a long way towards explaining the complete lack of moggy-related questions on the test, I now realized. He looked over the top of his specs. "Cassidy scored the highest mark we've ever seen at St Jude's. She's clearly a very special girl."

Mum threw Dad an amazed look, before leaning awkwardly towards me and planting a big kiss on my cheek. Dad seemed to be struggling to understand what he was hearing. But no one was more surprised than me to learn I was some kind of UNDISCOVERED GENIUS. Maybe I hadn't been guessing those answers at all; when I thought I'd been randomly picking A, B, C or D, my subconscious must have been guiding me towards the right answers without me even realizing it. Cor, who'd have thought?

"So you're not kicking me out, then?" I asked, feeling I ought to make sure I hadn't misunderstood what was being said.

"Of course not," Mr Archer said. "We've got high hopes for you, Cassidy. I think you are capable of great things."

Wow. I'd never been anything more than average at school before. I stared at the sheet of paper in Mr Archer's hand. It definitely had my name at the top. Maybe all those SUPER-BRAINFOOD FISH FINGERS were paying off after all.

"Wowzers," I replied faintly and then decided that it probably wasn't the kind of word someone with my IQ should use. What might a genius say when they found out they were the cleverest kid in school? Something highbrow and ultra witty, no doubt. "SUPER –" I began, before the part of my brain which had done such an excellent job of hiding my genius kicked in – "CALIFRAGILISTICEXPIALIDOCIOUS!"

I saw Mr Archer's eyes slide to my test results once again and a slight frown creased his forehead. Then he seemed to give his head a brisk shake and stood up, in a way that made it clear that the meeting was over. "Er... quite. Well said."

As he showed us out of his office, he waffled on about putting me forward for the Gifted and Talented programme and I kind of tuned out. US GENIUSESES... GENI-EYE...clever people cannot be expected to pay constant attention and I was too busy working out what difference my new brains were going to make in my everyday life to care about the boring stuff. I mean obviously, I'd be able to work out the square root of numbers like eighty-one without even trying (it's nine – see? SEE?) but there'd be other side-effects, too. Liam was in for a shock, that was for sure; he'd always claimed I was a few power-chords short of an anthem in the past. Molly and Shenice would be just as gobsmacked as me, although at least it meant I wouldn't be on my own in lessons now.

"Well done, Cassie," Dad said and I realized he was thinking about ruffling my hair. I dodged out of the way, right into the path of Mum.

"I think this calls for a celebratory tea tonight," she said, giving my shoulders a squeeze. "I'm sure Liam won't mind missing band practice just this once."

And there it was; the proof that BABY BRAIN is a

bona fide medical condition. Because if Mum thought Liam would willingly give up a **WOLF BRETHREN** rehearsal with the talent contest looming, then she hadn't just lost the plot, she'd misplaced the entire book. He was going to strop on an epic scale, especially when he found out what, exactly, we were celebrating. I grinned in anticipation and resisted the urge to rub my hands together in an evil-genius style. Being declared a **BRAINBOX** wasn't half bad so far. And there was another upside to being outed as the smartest girl in school; Nathan Crossfield was about to find out who I was, big time.

Don't tell anyone I said this, but sometimes it's not so terrible being me.

Dear Miss Bond,

Thank you for your letter dated 15th September in which you suggest a return to the Victorian school leaving age. I am sorry that you feel being forced to attend school is a "cruel and unusual punishment" and I can assure you that the Prime Minister does not make laws simply to "suck the fun out of EVERYTHING", as you suggest.

While I fully believe your claim that a career in a coal-mine would be preferable to double maths with Mr Peterson, I am afraid that there are very few working mines left in Great Britain and an eleven year old would regrettably not be allowed to dig for coal, no matter how handy with a toffee hammer they are. Perhaps it would be easier to ask Mr Peterson to make your lessons a little more interesting?

I have passed on your suggestion that the Prime Minister would be more "urban" with a fauxhawk.

Thank you once again for taking the time to write.

Yours faithfully,
Nicola Pemberton
Secretary to the Prime Minister

CHAPTER SEVEN

I never thought I'd say this but Molly is beginning to get on my nerves. Thursday is normally the day she has her singing lesson but she ditched it to invite herself round to my house after school, for the **THIRD TIME** this week. She said it was to work on our English assignment together but she spends so much time staring at the big family photo we had taken last year that I'd be **AMAZED** if she gets anything done. And it makes me feel a bit awkward too, because when it's just me and Molly, it feels like we're leaving Shenice out. I know I'd hate it if I found out they'd been doing stuff without me, even if it was just homework. I've decided that if Molly suggests coming over again tomorrow, I'm totally inviting Shen.

Anyway, it became obvious why Molly was really interested in hanging out at my house and it wasn't anything to do with my HILARIOUS HAMSTER IMPRESSION. As soon as Liam sauntered through the front door, her attitude changed. Honestly, it was like I'd suddenly ceased to exist. She pretended to be concentrating on her work but I could see her watching him from underneath her curls. He passed us without speaking, presumably on his way to the fridge, and from the look on her face, I guessed she was torn between PLAYING IT COOL and wanting to speak. She bottled it, though, and he went into the kitchen without so much as a grunt our way. Rolo, who'd been rolling around attacking my socks, jumped up and lolloped after him.

Molly fixed the kitchen door with the kind of intense, slightly cross-eyed stare the dog uses on his food bowl at teatime. I resisted the urge to smack her one with my ruler, although a good hard blow to the head may be just what she needs to get this ridiculous crush out of her system. Instead, I pretended I hadn't noticed she looked like she was about to WET HER PANTS. Anyway, whatever she did to psych herself up must have worked because when he came back from the kitchen (carrying a plate laden with two Crunchies, a family-sized packet of crisps and the last Cheese String – Mum was going to flip when she realized all her pregnancy essentials were gone), she grabbed her opportunity. "Hi, Liam."

Her voice was raspy and slightly American-sounding. I'm sure she intended to be ALLURING but she sounded like she had TONSILITIS.

Liam looked up and noticed us for the first time.

"Hey, if it isn't my number-one fan. How are you, Milly?"

She went red and I waited for her to indignantly point out that he'd got her name wrong. It didn't happen. Instead, she fanned her cheeks and smiled so hard that I swear her dimples got dimples. "I'm good. How are you? Everything cool with the band?"

I couldn't believe it – this was Molly, who'd once had a hissy fit when a girl in our class had spelled her name with an "ie" at the end in her Christmas card. Was she really going to let Liam, who had technically known her for about seven years, get away with calling her by completely the wrong name? Apparently she was.

Oblivious, Liam winked at her. "Believe. We can count on your vote in ST JUDE'S HAS GOT TALENT, right?"

Molly blushed. Again. Then she actually giggled. "It's all yours. WOLF BRETHREN ROCK!"

I couldn't help myself; I made a retching noise and pretended to throw up down the back of the sofa. Molly fired an accusing glare at me. I glared right back. I mean, I'm all for backing up my besties and everything but it's BECAUSE she's my BFF that I have to stop her from making an idiot of herself. Seriously, what does she see in Liam? And does she really think WOLF BRETHREN – ahem – ROCK? I know they reckon love is blind but this case it must be deaf as well. Me and Shenice are going to have to do something about this. I'm not sure what but it's our duty as BFFs to save her from herself. She'll thank us one day.

Liam ignored me and cocked his fingers at Molly. "Spread the word. And remember, the wolves are on the prowl."

He let out a low growl, which might not have seemed quite so dorky if the plate in his hand hadn't wobbled, causing the growl to become a yelp. He grabbed at the snacks before they fell on the floor. I laughed, earning myself a furious scowl from both directions.

"Those NEW SHOES you got a few weeks ago – they were black with red bits, weren't they?" Liam asked, once he'd regained control of his munchables.

I nodded, curiosity worming through me. It wasn't like Liam to notice anything about me, least of my shoes. "Yeah. Why?"

He started to climb the stairs, a strange smile on his face. "No reason."

Frowning, I tried to work out what his point was. He couldn't really be interested in my footwear so what was he getting at? My gaze slid down to the rug, where I'd kicked my shoes off earlier. Instead of two shiny ballet pumps, there was only one.

"What have you done with it?" I squeaked, even though I knew it couldn't have been him.

He carried on up the stairs and disappeared from view. "I haven't done anything with it," his voice floated down. "But you might want to check out what Rolo is chewing in the garden."

Groaning, I jumped to my feet and ran for the back door. Why is it always my stuff Rolo trashes? Liam's room is like an **ALADDIN'S CAVE** of half-eaten toast crusts and wax-encrusted hairbrushes; why can't Rolo unleash his destructive tendencies on those? Mum would go nutso if he destroyed another pair of my shoes and I knew the fact that Liam hadn't done a thing to stop him wouldn't make any difference. I'D still be dead meat.

"Don't just sit there – come and help me!" I yelled at Molly.

To my mild shock, she leaped up and followed me straight out. I half expected her to go chasing up the stairs — maybe she wasn't totally Team Liam after all. But even with her help, it still took an exhausting twenty-five minutes to catch Rolo. He thinks it is the GREATEST GAME EVER to let someone get within touching distance of his brown fur and then race off to another part of the garden, his tongue lolloping out like he is CRACKING UP. I thought dogs were supposed to be man's best friend but they don't behave like any best friend I've ever had — I'd be pretty annoyed if Molly or Shenice ate my shoes and threw up on my bed all the time. I am going to make him watch 101 DALMATIONS on loop until he learns how proper dogs behave.

To top it all, when we finally caught him he didn't even have my shoe — I found it under the sofa later. Glaring up at the house, I saw Liam watching from his bedroom window. He did this mocking slow handclap thing. I threw Molly a SEE-WHAT-I-HAVE-TO-PUT-UP-WITH look but she pretended not to notice, which stung a little bit. So she

STILL thought Liam was the WORLD'S BEST BROTHER, did she? If this little episode didn't show her what he was really like, nothing would. She was beyond help.

Oh. Em. Gee. Breathe. And breathe again. You will not BELIEVE what happened today. I'm not really sure I do and I was there. Nathan Crossfield knows I EXIST. He knows my name. And he actually spoke to me!

Mr Bearman asked me to stay behind after English and asked if I would consider joining the Year Seven quiz team. Nathan was on his way out of the class and Mr Bearman called him back to introduce us.

"Cassidy, meet Nathan, the captain of our team," Mr Bearman said. "Nathan, this is Cassie. Fingers crossed she'll be the fourth cog in our machine."

Nathan smiled and I felt my knees wobble a bit. "Hi, Cassie, I've heard a lot about you," he said warmly.

"I hope you're up for joining us — Royal Windsor Prep School reckon they've got it in the bag and I'd love to prove them wrong."

EEK, who had been talking about me and what had he heard? Then the realization dawned on me; he meant he'd heard about my CAT score. He couldn't know that I'd never been much good at quizzes, or that breezing my way through some school tests didn't change anything. What if I fluffed a crucial quiz question and embarrassed myself in front of everyone? But Nathan was studying me with his smoky blue eyes and I reminded myself that this was the perfect way for me to get to know him. Besides, wasn't I thinking about performing in a talent contest, without the slightest hint of an actual talent? That ranked much higher on the SHAME-O-METER. Maybe being clever was the thing I was good at and this was my chance to make sure everybody knew it. True, I'd have to brush up on my general knowledge but at least I could stop trying to recall the lost art of hula-hooping. If all else failed, I'd have to fall back on my wit and stun Nathan with hilarity. Hmmm. Perhaps I shouldn't put the hula hoop away just yet.

"So how about it, Cassie?" Nathan went on and I realized I was gawping at him like I was a few stars short of a galaxy. "Are you in?"

Oh, who was I kidding? He'd had me at "Hi, Cassie". I nodded. "Yeah, why not?"

He smiled then and I knew I'd made the right choice. So what if I had to read a few Wiki pages and learn the capital of Kazakhstan? I'd be hanging out with the coolest boy in our year. Seriously, what could possibly go wrong?

Ways to Impress Nathan

1. Do bust enhancement exercises every day. Shenice went up two bra sizes in the summer and Mum is still making me wear vests.
   Must persuade her to buy me a bra.

2. Makeover – like Sandy in GREASE but without the yucky cigarette and slinky top (see item 1).

3. Get amazing new hairstyle. Or a wig. ♡

4. Wow him with amazing little-known facts.
   Will need to find out little-known facts first –
   do not think naming the entire Droids back-catalogue will work. May need a new notebook.
   And glitter pens.

CHAPTER EIGHT

Talking to my mother at the moment is like trying to negotiate a stretch of ground strewn with landmines. Seriously, she is pricklier than PRICKLY THE HEDGEHOG sitting on a thistle patch. It's October now and if she is going to be like this until Christmas then I may need to leave home – I cannot take another two months of her moods. After Sunday lunch, I made the mistake of asking if I could get blonde highlights – you would think I had asked for diamond-tipped extensions the way she went on.

"Do you have any idea how much they cost?" she ranted, after what felt like a lifetime of lip pursing and huffing. "Even if you were old enough, which you're not, there's the maintenance to consider. The roots need to be done every six weeks. Honestly, I don't know what's got into you lately. You know money is tight at the moment."

I am beginning to think that the twins are forcing us below the poverty line. If she didn't insist on buying every baby product on the market then maybe we wouldn't be flat broke. I mean, how many SLEEPSUITS can two little people need? I reckon we'll have enough stuff to open our own branch of Mothercare soon. I opened my mouth to suggest that she considered the needs of her other children once in a while but the words died in my throat. Who needs hairdressers, anyway? I thought, as I stamped up the stairs to my bedroom. It's Molly's turn to have a sleepover this Friday, I'll just buy a highlighter kit on the way home from school and get them to apply it. My mother cannot complain that I'm costing too much then, can she?

School is a completely different place now that I am a SOMEBODY. All the teachers seem to know my name, even the ones who don't teach me. And being on speaking terms with Nathan seems to have made the rest of my year view me with a bit more respect, although not all of them are impressed with my quiz team status. I caught Imani Willis giving me a STINKY-EYED STARE in English this morning when Nathan stopped to remind me about the first meeting of the quiz team next week. Shenice says it's because she fancies him and sees me as a threat. I'm not sure about that because Imani is gorgeous and could easily pass for fourteen. Maybe once the girls have turned me from MOUSE to SUN-KISSED BLONDE tonight, I will feel differently.

"It says here that in forty-five minutes, you'll have the lavish colour you always dreamed of," Shenice said, peering at the instruction sheet in her hand. "You did do a sensitivity test, didn't you?"

We were sandwiched into Molly's bathroom. The contents of the highlighting kit were laid out on the windowsill and I had a greying old towel wrapped around my shoulders. Molly had a plastic brush thing in one hand and what looked suspiciously like a crochet hook in the other. Shenice was in charge of reading the instructions to make sure we followed them to the letter.

I nodded and held back my hair for her to check. "Yep, behind my ear two days ago. I didn't have a reaction to any of the ingredients."

"Good. I read this story about a woman who hadn't done a patch test and she was allergic." Shenice paused and lowered her voice to a hoarse whisper. "SHE DIED."

Molly waved the crochet hook. "This looks like those things the Egyptians used to pull your brains out of your nose once you were dead."

I took it off her. "I'm not letting you anywhere near me with that. It says the plastic applicator gives bolder, more striking results. Besides, you'd probably impale my head with it."

Shenice finished studying the sheet of paper and pulled on the rubber gloves. "Right. Are you ready?"

She screwed the plastic applicator onto the bottle of bleachy-smelling liquid and passed it to Molly, who was wearing a pair of bright-yellow Marigolds she'd found under the sink.

"I hope you don't clean the loo wearing those,"
I said.

Molly sniffed, then shrugged. "From the smell coming out of this bottle, I don't think you need to worry about stray bacteria from the loo." She adopted a gravelly voice. "RADIANT BLONDE HIGHLIGHT KIT kills all known germs dead."

Shenice checked the time. "Okay, let's get started. Commence OPERATION BLONDE BOMBSHELL."

The first gloop of cold gel on my scalp stung a bit. By the time all the dye had been applied, my head was burning. "Erm...is it meant to hurt?"

Shenice consulted the instructions. "It says a tingling sensation might be experienced."

That was some tingle. But no pain, no gain. Carefully,

I tipped my head to check my watch. "Right. How long do I need to leave it on for?"

Molly checked the stopwatch on her phone, frowning. "Well according to this, you've got three minutes left but that can't be right because we only just applied the stuff to the back of your head."

Shenice turned the sheet of paper over. "It says here to leave for no longer than forty-five minutes. Maybe it works faster on the back bits."

All three of us studied my reflection in the mirror. A trickle of dye was snaking towards my chin and my forehead looked like I had an OOMPA-LOOMPA somewhere in my family tree. My hair itself was a mass of slimy mud-coloured strands plastered to my head. Overall, it wasn't a look that screamed glamour and sophistication.

"So we'll give it a little bit longer, then?" I ventured, wiping away the streak on my cheek and hoping the distinct orangey line would vanish with soap and water.

Molly snapped off her gloves. "Come on. Let's have a game of SINGSTAR while we wait."

By the time we'd trooped into her room and each sung a song, twenty minutes had gone by and we were all itching (in my case, quite literally) to see the results of our handiwork. Back in the bathroom, I tipped my head upside down over the bath and waited while my personal beauticians rinsed the dye away.

"Well?" I demanded, once the water had stopped cascading over my ears. "How does it look?"

There was a long silence.

"Well, the packet does say it gives MULTI-TONAL HIGHLIGHTS," Shenice said eventually, and her voice only quavered a little bit.

"Shenice, they're GINGER," I heard Molly hiss. "And those ones at the front look GREEN."

Suddenly filled with a sense of impending doom, I leaped up and stared at my reflection. Sure enough, there were several different colours highlighting my previously ordinary hair, ranging from DIRTY GREYISH BLONDE through to an unmistakeable POND-SLUDGE GREEN. But that wasn't the worst of it; on the crown of my head, the highlights merged together to form a huge, uneven blob of brassy orange. It looked like someone had smashed an egg onto my skull. I let out a HORROR-STRUCK WAIL and covered my eyes. "Make it go away!"

Shenice dabbed at my head with a towel, her face

pale. "It's probably the light in here. I'm sure it'll look better once your hair is dry."

I peered out through my fingers, hoping it wasn't as bad as it had looked, then clamped my eyes shut again – if anything, it was worse. And to top it all, Molly's mum must have heard my scream and had come up to investigate. She thudded on the bathroom door. "What's going on in there?"

"Don't let her in," I begged Molly in a whisper. "She can't see me like this!"

"Nothing," Molly called out, sounding panicky even to my dye-stained ears. "We're getting ready for bed, that's all."

"Don't give me that rubbish, Molly, it's only eight-thirty," her mum replied, her voice ringing with suspicion. "Open the door, please. I want to know what that smell is."

Molly threw me a SORROWFUL LOOK but I knew she had no choice. She reached over and tugged back the bolt. The door swung open to reveal Mrs Papadopoulos standing on the landing. She took one look at my stricken head and put both hands to her mouth.

"I knew you were up to no good. Your mother is going to kill you." Her eyes took in the state of the bathroom. Globules of dye adorned every surface, including the toilet bowl. "And if she doesn't, I will!"

CHAPTER NINE

The plan was to get home early and sneak upstairs
without anyone seeing me on Saturday morning. But
Molly's mum had already sent an apologetic text to mine,
explaining she'd had no idea what we were doing until it was
too late, so there was the exact opposite of a welcoming
committee awaiting me when I pushed back the front
door and stepped into our hallway.

"Cassidy Bond, get in here. Now."

Mum sounded so grim that I knew ignoring her was not an option. I'd have to try to brazen it out. Taking a deep breath, I pushed open the living-room door.

"Hey," I said, as innocently as I could manage. "What's up?"

"Cold out, is it?" Dad asked, gesturing at the RED BOBBLE HAT I had jammed down over my ears.

"It is October," I pointed out, defensively. "There's a bit of a nip in the air, since you ask."

Mum looked on in stony silence. Dad eyed me sympathetically.

"Better just to get it over with, Cassie," he said kindly. "Like tearing off a plaster."

There was no escape. Feeling hunted, I reluctantly reached for my head.

Mum's face was a PICTURE OF HORROR when I pulled off Molly's hat and my TECHNICOLOURED hair tumbled out. Dad, on the other hand, burst out laughing. Liam almost spat his drink everywhere.

"What have you done to yourself, you idiot girl?" Mum demanded in a strangled tone, once she'd recovered the power of speech.

I thought it was pretty obvious what I'd done but perhaps now wasn't the time for sarcasm. "It didn't look like this on the box."

That sent Dad off into a fresh gale of laughter. Mum threw him an exasperated look. "If you want to do something useful, you can go and fetch the scissors. It's going to have to come off."

Liam let out a GLEE-FILLED CACKLE as Dad went to the kitchen. I felt every last drop of blood drain from my face. Was she being serious?

"I th-thought we could j-just dye it again," I stammered, searching her set expression for the faintest hint she was winding me up as part of my punishment.

She laid a protective hand over her bump, frowning. "I can't. Even with gloves on, it wouldn't be good for the babies." Casting a critical eye over my hair, she sighed. "Besides, it would need a professional hairdresser to sort that mess out and we simply cannot afford it. Better to cut it as short as we can and let the rest grow out."

"I'll do it," Liam offered, grinning. "I can use my clippers. I reckon she'd look good with an all-over grade one."

The problem was that I couldn't tell if Mum and Liam

were serious. My lower lip began to WOBBLE at the thought of turning up at school on Monday with no hair. I'd be a laughing stock.

Dad's voice drifted through from the kitchen. "Cassie, come here and help me look."

Blinking back tears, I trudged past my cruel mother and sadistic brother.

"If you love me at all, you'll make sure she cuts my entire head off," I told Dad miserably. "It would be kinder."

He patted me on the shoulder. "It's not that bad. I've got a LOVELY ELVIS WIG you can borrow if you want to?"

Fresh tears threatened to spill down my cheeks. "Dad!" I wailed. "You're not helping!"

"Sorry," he said, and his amusement faded a bit. He jangled the car keys in front of my face. "Why don't we sneak out the back and see if any of the hairdressers in town can fit you in?"

It's not often I am moved to physical contact where my parents are concerned but I threw my arms around Dad and hugged him. "Yes. YES! Let's go!"

Grinning, he ruffled MY TORTURED HAIR and, for once, I didn't try to squirm out of the way.

"Just do me one favour, Cassie," he said as I followed him out of the back door.

Here it came – the KILLER CONDITION which meant I'd be washing his car for the rest of my days or bringing him tea and toast in bed every weekend for all eternity. "Yes?"

He tugged Molly's bobble hat out of my hand, chuckling. "Wear this and keep your head down, eh?"

Mum would be furious when she realized where we'd gone, but by then it would be too late for her to wield the CLIPPERS OF DOOM. Maybe today wouldn't be such a bad day after all.

CHAPTER TEN

I never thought I'd say this but my dad officially ROCKS. Not only did he manage to find a hairdresser who could sort out my DISASTROUS HAIR, he took me to one who actually managed to make me look better than I've ever done before. And he paid the HIDEOUSLY EXPENSIVE bill without a single comment, which somehow made me feel even guiltier. I will have to find some way to repay him.

It turns out I wasn't born to be a blonde, as I'd always thought. Underneath my mousy brown lurked a glossy brunette and all it took was an hour and a half with Sheryl from Hair Apparent on Peascod Street to bring it out. She also snipped the damaged straggly bits into cute flicky-out layers. I couldn't stop checking them out and even Mum grudgingly admitted that it looked good.

"Not that you deserve it," she sniffed over our Sunday roast. "By rights, you should be BALDER than DUNCAN GOODHEW."

I don't know why she expects any of us to know who these people are. Even Dad doesn't recognize some of the names she comes out with. Sometimes I think she makes them up. And what kind of mother wants her daughter to be bald, anyway? The pregnancy hormones are turning her into the EVIL QUEEN from SNOW WHITE.

Dad caught my eye and winked at me over her head. I smiled back and we had this odd flash of understanding. It comes to something when your dad gets you better than your mum. The next thing I know, Liam will be telling me he's got my back. HA HA HA HA.

As though reading my mind, Liam frowned at me. "Your hair reminds me of someone but I can't work out who it is." He thought for a minute, then snapped his fingers and grinned. "Got it – Rolo!"

Huh, that was a bit rich coming from someone with a fringe like an old English sheepdog. But the new improved Cassidy Bond is a CLASSY GIRL and she doesn't trade insults with moronic older brothers. So I simply smiled and imagined myself shaving his eyebrows off while he slept.

When I got upstairs, I looked Duncan Goodhew up and discovered that he is some swimmer from centuries ago who had no hair at all, not even any eyebrows or eyelashes. I cannot believe Mum would have made me look like him just to prove a point. If she thinks I am making her breakfast in bed next Mother's Day, she can forget it.

I bet EINSTEIN'S mother never threatened to shave his head.

School on Monday was such a BUZZ. Girls I'd never spoken to before stopped me to ask where I'd got my hair done and, rather scarily, a Year Ten boy WOLF-WHISTLED at me and his mate HOWLED like a dog. I think it was meant to be a compliment but it made me feel a bit weird. I mean, this must be what it's like to be popular – you're never invisible. It wasn't so bad once I'd got used to it, although I could do without the peculiar boy behaviour.

In fact, I'm almost glad the highlight kit went so spectacularly wrong. And I owe Dad big time for saving me from the clippers. Molly and Shenice reckon Mum wouldn't have gone through with it. I'm not so sure.

Molly's OBSESSION with my PIG OF A BROTHER seems to be getting worse. She spent almost her entire lunch break today handing out WOLF BRETHREN flyers and begging people to like their Facebook page. Shenice agrees with me that Liam is just using her but doesn't have any idea what to do to open her eyes. If my story about him chewing his own toenails didn't put her off, I don't know what will. I'm pretty sure Liam and his mates are making jokes behind her back, too, but they're tolerating her while she's useful. It's all going to end in tears once SJHGT is over and you can bet your Converse they won't be my brother's.

The thing is, it kind of feels like Molly is doing her own fair share of using at the moment. The first thing she asks when I invite her over is whether Liam is home and she spends all her time distracted, jumping every time a door opens like she's waiting to catch a glimpse of him. Shenice says we should say something but I don't want to antagonize her. An angry Molly is a SCARY thing.

With a bit of luck, Liam will do something extraordinarily gross soon and she'll wonder what she ever saw in him.

I had BUTTERFLIES in my tummy when I pushed open the door of the library for the first meeting of the quiz team after school. What would Nathan make of the new me? Would he even notice? And what would the other team members be like?

"Ah, there you are, Cassie," Mr Bearman called. "Come and take a seat, and meet the rest of TEAM ST JUDE'S."

Trying to ignore the fluttering inside me, I sat down at the table. There were four of us – Nathan, me and another boy and girl I didn't know. Both of the other kids looked serious. The girl had tiny black-rimmed glasses and a really severe ponytail. The boy looked so intense that I wouldn't mind betting he did Sudoku in his sleep, and I'm not talking about the easy ones.

"This is Rebecca, and this is Bilal." Mr Bearman introduced each of them. "And, of course, you already know Nathan."

Nathan smiled. "Cassie is our secret weapon against Royal Windsor Prep," he told the other two and I cringed inside, thinking about my mum's less-than-complimentary comments at the weekend. But Rebecca and Bilal couldn't have any idea about my scatty behaviour or embarrassing secret. All they saw was an asset to the team. Hopefully, with really great hair.

Rebecca nodded a blank-faced greeting. "We were just about to divide up the areas for revision," she said, pen poised over a thick notebook. "What's your specialist subject?"

Now there was a question no one had ever asked me before. I suppose I was meant to say something highbrow, like the ROMAN EMPIRE or ELEMENTS OF

THE PERIODIC TABLE, but my mind went blank and I blurted out the first thing that came into it. "Er... Harry Potter?"

Rebecca's pen hovered over the page as she stared at me and I thought about cracking a "Just kidding!" smile. But Mr Bearman was nodding hard.

"Always handy to have a reader on the team," he said in a cheerful tone. "There's bound to be a question or two about He Who Must Not Be Named in the literature round."

Rebecca dropped her gaze and began to write. I heaved a sigh of relief and decided I should probably start reading the books again. Or at least watch the films. The last thing I wanted to do was show myself up in front of Nathan. Rebecca's specialist subject was MYTHOLOGY and Bilal was some kind of NATURAL HISTORY expert, whatever that is. Nathan said he was more of an

ALL-ROUNDER and I could have kicked myself. Why didn't I think of that?

Mr Bearman explained that the quiz is split into rounds against local schools, with a regional heat which leads to the national final. In our first official outing as a team, we'll be up against twelve other schools, including the scary-sounding Royal Windsor, and that is just after half-term — only five weeks away. As well as our weekly Monday after-school sessions, he suggested we try to meet up in the half-term holiday to go over practice tests and identify any last-minute weaknesses.

"So where are we going to meet?" Nathan asked. "Anyone got any ideas?"

Before anyone else could speak, my hand was in the air. "You can come over to my house," I said, hoping I didn't sound as pathetically keen as I felt. "As long as you don't mind dogs."

Mr Bearman looked pleased. "Thanks, Cassie. Perhaps you could check that it's okay with your parents and let the others know?"

I nodded, hoping Mum wouldn't mind them coming over. She'd never complained about having Molly and Shenice round in the past, but she'd be even more pregnant by then and her moods were unpredictable enough now. Maybe she wouldn't want a houseful, even if it was for the good of my education. I'd have to do something with Rolo, too. He'd probably try to eat one of the others if I didn't think of somewhere for him to go.

The meeting wrapped up shortly after that. As we were leaving, Nathan fell into step beside me. "Thanks for offering to have us round your house," he said. "I'm really glad you're on the team."

I felt the start of a BLUSH creeping up my cheeks. "No worries."

He held open the library door and we stopped outside. There was a bit of an AWKWARD SILENCE.

"So, I'll see you around, then?" he said, raising his eyebrows.

"Yeah," I replied, feeling a stab of disappointment that he hadn't noticed my new look. "See you."

I got about ten steps away before he called out my name. "Cassie?"

I turned around. "Yeah?"

He flashed a grin at me. "Looking good."

This time, there was no stopping my face from turning red. I spun around so that he wouldn't see. "Thanks. You're not so bad yourself."

Okay, so it's not going to win me the **NOBEL PRIZE FOR COMEBACKS** but I don't care. Nathan Crossfield thinks I look good and that, for now, is all that matters.

Ten Freaky
Animal Facts

* Giraffes can lick their own ears — huh. Show-offs...

* Emus cannot walk backwards.

* An octopus can eat its own arm if it gets stressed — know how it feels.

* A leech has thirty-two brains — may recruit one for Team St Jude's.

* Tarantulas can live for thirty years.

* The most common bird in the world is the chicken.

* A slug has four noses. How does it smell? Terrible! (This joke may need work.)

* Cats have over a hundred vocal sounds, dogs only have about ten.

* Oysters can change gender.

* There are more than 2400 species of flea in the world — yuck!

CHAPTER ELEVEN

So, today scores about a 9.5 on the SUCK-O-METER. To start off with, I was tossing and turning all night and the only reason I know that I fell asleep at all was that I had a bad dream in which I was walking around school in MY UNDERWEAR and people were firing random questions at me. It doesn't take a degree in dream interpretation to figure out what that's all about — with less than three weeks to go until the quiz team regional heats, the pressure is building and I get the feeling Bilal and Rebecca don't really understand what I bring to the table. So it's not a massive surprise that I am a teensy bit stressed about it all. It took me ages to drag myself out of bed and when I did, I discovered that cute flicky-out layers are not so easy when you are in a rush and all you have to use is a broken comb and a travel hairdryer. Bring on next week, when I can sleep in as long as I like and it doesn't matter if I look like a SNAKE-HAIRED mess.

Mum was being her usual understanding self.

"Get a move on, Cassie," she bellowed up the stairs as I was desperately slapping Liam's wax onto my wayward hair, which made it look like a slug had dissolved on my head. "You're going to school, not London Fashion Week."

For someone who claims to get breathless just walking to the car, she hasn't half got a loud shout. I wonder sometimes if she exaggerates the symptoms of pregnancy so that we all feel sorry for her. Then again,

I accidentally caught a bit of **ONE BORN EVERY MINUTE** last night and now that I know what she's going to have to do, I think she deserves my sympathy. Why do women ever have more than one baby? **EWWWW.** Although obviously I'm glad my parents didn't stop at one or I wouldn't exist. Liam probably wishes they had.

Anyway, I can't afford to get in Mum's bad books because I keep forgetting to ask if **TEAM SJ** can come round to study in the holidays, and there are only three days left until we break up. On Monday night she was out at her yoga class, and last night she fell asleep in front of the TV. Dad wouldn't let me wake her so I haven't had a chance to ask yet. I'm sure she won't mind but I'm not jinxing it by telling Nathan we're good to go until the **FAT LADY** nods. Besides, I'd rather not get too close to him with my hair looking like I've just landed from **PLANET SLIME**.

Liam took one look at me as I got in the car and shook his head. "Adopted, remember?"

I wonder sometimes if he's the one who is adopted. It would explain so much.

In spite of all that, the day wouldn't have sucked quite so badly if it hadn't been for the GINORMOUS argument I had with Molly. We've been planning to go trick or treating on Halloween for months and now she says she can't go because she has "other commitments".
I know she is practising a song for SJHGT but surely that doesn't take up twenty-four-seven? And I bet she could take one night off if she really wanted to. That's when I discovered the real reason she didn't want to go – WOLF BRETHREN were rehearsing and Liam had invited her to watch them, presumably to keep her sweet and make sure she kept on doing their running around for them.
I don't know what annoyed me more – the fact that she'd dumped me and Shenice AGAIN or that she is

TOO STUPID to see what Liam's real motives are.

"Does he know you're entering the contest?" I demanded, confronting her on the way home from school.

She thrust her chin in the air. "Yes. I told him ages ago."

I snorted, trying not to feel weird that she seemed to communicate more with my brother than I did. "I'd double-check if I were you. How do you think he's going to react when you wipe the floor with his stupid band in the competition?"

"Well, maybe I'll pull out, then," she declared. "The band is more important than me."

I stared at her, wishing Shenice hadn't had to go to a swim team meeting so that she could hear the RUBBISH Molly was coming out with. "Okay, who are you and what have you done with my friend? The Molly Papadopoulos I know would never say something like that."

"We're not all as ME-ME-ME as you, Cassie," she fired back. "Just because I don't think winning is the be-all and end-all, you think I've gone mental."

Me-me-me – er...ME? That was a bit rich coming from the person who was choosing a CRUMMY BAND over her BEST FRIENDS. And how had this suddenly become about me, anyway? I was just an innocent bystander. Besides, the last time I checked, Liam was way more self-absorbed than I was. I gritted my teeth. "No, I think you're putting my waste-of-space brother first when he doesn't deserve it."

She tossed her head. "You don't see what I see."

I wanted to slap her, I really did. "Obviously," I snapped. "But don't expect any sympathy when he drops you like a stone after ST JUDE'S HAS GOT TALENT."

She eyed me coldly. "Jealousy is a terrible thing, Cassie. Just because Liam got all the talent, doesn't mean you have to hate on him all the time."

And that was when I really lost it. "You know what?" I exploded, peeling off down a side road so that I wouldn't have to look at her any more. "You deserve everything you get. And FYI, me and Shenice will be going trick or treating without you. We might actually enjoy ourselves without you banging on about WOLF BRETHREN the whole time, anyway."

I didn't wait to hear her reply. With angry tears filling my eyes, I stamped down the road. It wasn't until I got around the corner that I realized I'd gone down a cul-de-sac. But I couldn't go back out straight away because Molly might see me and think I wanted to apologize. So I sat on a garden wall to wait, replaying the argument in my head. Then an old lady came out and told me to shove off or she'd hit me with her broom, which was really unfair because I wasn't even doing anything. That's the last time I donate to the Age Concern lady outside Tesco.

Like I said, today is made of SUCKAGE.

More Quiz Queen Factoids

✳ Starfish have water for blood.

✳ Q is the only letter in the alphabet that does not appear in the name of any of the United States.

✳ Venus is the only planet that rotates clockwise – how do they know this stuff?

✳ Sharks have upper and lower eyelids, but they do not blink. Memo to self: do not play shark at poker.

✳ The lifespan of an eyelash is approximately 90 days.

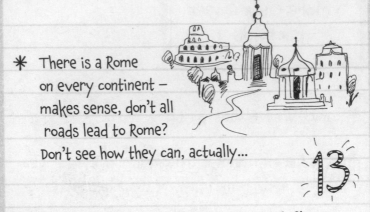

* There is a Rome on every continent — makes sense, don't all roads lead to Rome? Don't see how they can, actually...

* A lot of hotels avoid having a thirteenth floor.

* If you shouted for eight years, seven months and six days, you would produce enough sound energy to heat a cup of tea — unless you are my mother, in which case one dragon-esque roar will do it...

CHAPTER TWELVE

Shenice was totally on my side when I phoned her to explain what had happened. We both agreed that it was going to take something pretty drastic to force Molly to snap out of her obsession with Liam.

"Whatever happened to SISTERS before MISTERS?" Shenice asked, sounding aggrieved. "MATES before DATES?"

"BESTIES before BOYS," I agreed, although my mind

wasn't really on the conversation. Mostly, I was thinking how weird it will be going out on Halloween without Molly, but she has made her bed and it is with the SMELLY WOLVES. She's on her own from now on.

Mum was surprisingly keen to have the quiz team round in half-term. I think she has been worried that I would be bored and expect her to entertain me. Sometimes, I swear she thinks I am still four years old. But I wasn't complaining — I don't know where the first half-term at St Jude's went but we were suddenly only two weeks away from the quiz and we needed to do some serious cramming.

So, on Monday afternoon, Rebecca, Bilal and Nathan arrived at the house for our revision session. I hadn't mentioned that they were coming over to Liam — I decided that he was more likely to hang around if he knew there'd be an audience for him to show off to. And he'd try to turn them into WOLF BRETHREN fans. The thought of Rebecca and Bilal politely listening to their brand of shouty-shouty noise made me smile; I doubted either of them were big thrash metal fans. That wouldn't deter Liam, though. It would be safest if he was out of the house. Luckily, the GODS OF PUT-UPON LITTLE SISTERS were smiling on me for once and he announced to Mum that he was going to the park for a kick-about.

Briefly, I wondered if Molly would be there. I bet she would – for the last few days of term she'd resolutely ignored both me and Shenice. Not that we'd been falling over ourselves to speak to her. It felt strange, being a pair instead of a trio, but at least Shenice and I had each other. I'd seen Molly sitting on her own in the playground at breaks and lunchtime and knew she must be feeling lonely without us. I almost suggested we went over to see her. Then I remembered how she'd put Liam before us and stayed where I was.

Even so, I kind of MISSED Molly. We'd squabbled
and fought amongst ourselves before but never fallen out
completely and she didn't have any brothers or sisters to
rely on for company in the holidays. In a way, I could
hardly blame her for hanging around Liam.

I almost forgot about my problems with Molly once
Nathan and the others arrived, though. Mum was actually
quite sociable, waddling round offering
drinks and biscuits.

"I've got cashew nuts and bananas, if you're after
something a bit healthier," she twittered on as we sat
down in the living room. "And I thought you might like to
listen to one of my meditation CDs, to help you
concentrate."

Hang on, weren't those CDs for giving birth? I heard
muffled laughter coming from Rebecca and felt my cheeks
getting warm. Grabbing the remote control, I zapped the

TV into life. "It's okay. We'll have the music channel on. Stop fussing, Mum."

She fixed me with a level stare and I thought for one stomach-flipping moment that she was going to sit down with us. But then she sighed. "Fine, whatever works best for you. I'll be in the kitchen if you need anything."

"When is the baby due?" Nathan asked once the kitchen door had closed.

"BABIES," I corrected him, smiling. "TWINS, and they're due on Boxing Day."

Nathan's eyes widened. "Wow. How do you feel about them?"

It was a good question and the answer seemed to change on a daily basis. At the moment, I was feeling OKAY-ISH to our expanding family. "Excited, I suppose.

But worried I'll be expected to change nappies, obviously."

"I'd hate it if my mum had any more children," Rebecca said, shuddering. "I think I'd leave home."

I didn't want to admit that I'd felt the same at first. "Trust me, my older brother is way more annoying than the twins could ever be," I said. "He's about as much fun to have around as a DEMENTOR."

Nathan smiled. "Older sisters aren't much better. Mine spends half her life on her phone and the other half in the bathroom."

Mum came through from the kitchen and Rolo took the opportunity to bound through behind her. Tail wagging like he'd found some long-lost friends, he offered a slobbery greeting to my team-mates.

"Sorry," I said, firing a meaningful look at Mum. "He was supposed to stay in the kitchen."

Nathan ruffled Rolo's ears. "Don't worry, he can be our team mascot."

Bilal cleared his throat. "We should get started. There are loads of sample questions to get through."

"Ooh, do you need a quiz master?" Mum asked, her face brightening. "I do a brilliant Jeremy Paxman impression."

It's not brilliant, it's ABYSMAL, and she does it every time UNIVERSITY CHALLENGE is on. Imagine a heavily pregnant woman impersonating a middle-aged posh man and multiply the cringe-factor by a zillion. For one SICK-MAKING second, I thought she was actually going to launch into it. Then Nathan rescued me. "They're written questions, Mrs Bond. Thanks, anyway."

127

I flashed him a grateful look before glaring at my mother. "Can you take Rolo out with you, please? He's trying to eat the TV again."

Once Rolo had been dragged into the kitchen, we got down to business. I was surprised at how many of the answers I knew; maybe my research was starting to pay off. It wasn't until we swapped answer sheets that I realized I hadn't got as many right as I'd thought.

"The capital of the USA is Washington DC, not New York," Rebecca said with a tut. "I thought everyone knew that."

I squirmed in my seat. "Right. Of course it is."

She scowled over the top of her glasses at me. "The biggest animal on earth is the blue whale

and the Battle of Hastings was in 1066." Her eyes narrowed suspiciously. "Remind me how you got picked for the quiz team again?"

It was all right for them, the three of them had gone to the same primary school, the kind that encouraged competitive quizzes. Molly and Shenice and me had been too busy playing **POP STARS** for that. The blood began to roar in my ears. "Sorry."

"It doesn't matter if you get a few wrong," Nathan said, frowning at Rebecca. "We've all done these quizzes before, remember? Cassie hasn't."

The kitchen door swung open and Rolo barrelled in. I was so busy trying not to cry that I didn't pay him much attention as he dived under a chair, growling. Blinking, I concentrated on marking the last of Nathan's questions — twenty out of twenty. Glancing at the other sheets, I saw that Rebecca had got two wrong and Bilal one. My score was an accusatory eleven, written in ugly red pen on the paper in Rebecca's hand.

"I guess I've got some work to do," I offered, hoping my voice didn't sound as WOBBLY as I felt. For a SO-CALLED GENIUS, I didn't feel very clever.

"What is your dog chewing?" Rebecca asked, frowning at Rolo, who was half under the chair and tugging and gnawing at something pink and white with great enthusiasm. Her nose wrinkled with disgust. "Is it...a pair of KNICKERS?"

The embarrassment I felt at scoring so badly on the quiz evaporated instantly as a new kind of horror took hold. I almost didn't dare look. Diving towards Rolo, I tried to snatch whatever it was from his mouth but he thought I wanted to play and bounced away, tail beating the air. His latest "TOY" dangled from his mouth.

"No, Rolo," I groaned and grabbed for him. He leaped backwards, letting out a playful growl. Now I could see a leg hole and knew without a doubt that he'd got hold of a pair of pants. "Drop!"

He shook his head and pranced up and down with his prize. My patience ran out. "Rolo Bond, put that down this minute!" I bellowed.

With a whine, his ears flattened against his head and he dropped the knickers. And I realized how much I hadn't thought things through when they landed right beside Nathan's foot. In slow motion, I watched him stretch out a hand and pick them up. Then the FULL HORROR dawned. They weren't just any old pants – they were mine. And they had a fairy on the front.

Man's best friend? More like GIRL'S WORST NIGHTMARE.

Cassie's Fact-o-rama

✳ The chances of being killed by a dog are
1 in 700,000 – think they must
be a lot higher if you live with
Rolo, since you might easily
die of embarrassment...

✳ Elvis Presley never did a concert in the UK. Don't
worry. My father is making up for it.

✳ Crocodiles cannot stick their tongue out – guessing
this means they cannot lick their elbow either.
Told you it was a special talent.

* Butterflies taste with their feet.

* Scientists believe that the smarter you are, the more you dream. This explains why I have so many weird dreams.

* Your thumb is the same length as your nose — don't try this at home, accidentally poked myself in the eye trying to check it.

* Ants stretch when they wake up in the morning.

* It is against the law to sing off-key in North Carolina — wish it was in Windsor too, then Wolf Brethren would be arrested.

* Wales once held the record for the most people dressed up as a Smurf at any one time. What the WHAT?!

* Tongue prints are as unique as fingerprints!

CHAPTER THIRTEEN

Here we are again: Sunday evening. When we were in primary school, the holidays seemed to stretch on for ever — now that we are at St Jude's, half-term week has gone by in a flash. I am wondering if it's too late to join MI6 so that I can be sent on an **UNDERCOVER MISSION** and never have to go to school again. It doesn't matter how many times I replay **KNICKERGATE** in my head, it doesn't get any better and I cannot bear the thought of facing Nathan, Rebecca and Bilal at school tomorrow. It's like when I thought Mum was going to cut all my hair off,

except that there's no possible silver lining to owning
FAIRY UNDERWEAR.

On top of that, Molly is still not speaking to us.
I ended up spilling the whole story to Mum when she found
out it was just me and Shenice going trick or treating. She
got all cross and told me I should be the BIGGER PERSON
and make friends. But when I texted Molly, she ignored it
and I know she got the message. I wasn't sure what to do
then; was I supposed to just keep getting bigger and
bigger until she couldn't possibly ignore me? Shen and I
got dressed up in our HIPPOGRIFF costume anyway, and
went trick or treating without her. We did our best but it
wasn't the same without Molly in her HERMIONE outfit —
no one knew what we were supposed to be and one woman
thought we were GONZO from THE MUPPETS. And
although we giggled a lot, neither of us got the hysterical
can't-breathe-from-laughing feeling we usually get. But
we made a pact that if we ever make friends and Molly
asks us about it, we had the BEST NIGHT EVER. Even if I

did spend most of it with my face squashed against Shenice's back.

As if I wasn't enough of a STRESS-HEAD over Molly, I'm also fretting about my performance in the quiz. I'm clearly not as knowledgeable as the others, even though I've sat up really late every night reading Wikipedia and have learned all kinds of stuff. Who knew that seahorses can see behind them and in front of them at the same time? But what if I get a key question wrong and mess everything up? Then I'll be the girl with the pant-munching dog who ruined their chances of getting to the next round. I'll never live it down.

I might tell Mr Bearman that I'm quitting the team. That kills two of my worries with one stone. It won't help with Molly but I'm not sure what else to do with her. The ball is in her court.

I coughed and I coughed until I thought I might actually throw up on Monday morning but Mum still REFUSED to believe I have MALARIA. She just rolled her eyes and told me to get in the car. Honestly, what do I have to do to get the day off school?

I managed to make it through to lunchtime without meeting any of the quiz team. And then my luck didn't so much run out as SMASH the HUNDRED METRES WORLD RECORD, because the one person I didn't want to see was the one I bumped into. Quite literally, it turned out, in the canteen. And school canteen moussaka and water down the front of your blouse isn't a good look. In case you were wondering.

Nathan was really apologetic. "I'm really sorry, Cassie," he said, as I picked bits of aubergine off my legs and dropped them onto my empty plate. "I should have been watching where I was going."

"No, it was my fault," I sighed, dabbing at the spreading orange stain on my blouse. Typically, he'd had an empty plate and didn't have a mark on him. It was the story of my life.

"Did you have a good holiday? After – after Rolo..." He trailed off.

"They were old pants, you know. I haven't worn them for years," I said defensively. There was an awkward silence while I cursed my tendency to OVER-SHARE. Then I did what I always do when faced with a yawning chasm in the conversation; I tried to fill it. "Did you know that Belgium has a museum dedicated to strawberries?"

Nathan smiled. "I didn't know that. Have you been brushing up on your general knowledge or are strawberries a passion of yours?"

Willing my burning cheeks to cool down, I smiled back.

"Brushing up. I don't want to let the team down, after all."

Shenice tugged at my arm. "Cass—"

I ignored her. Nathan looked pleased that I'd been working hard for the team. "Good." Nodding at my blouse, he added, "I'm no expert but I don't think that's going to come out."

He was right – in spite of the full glass of water I'd been carrying doing its best to dilute the stain, the blouse looked awful and was beyond saving. I'd have to wear my PE shirt and hope none of the teachers noticed.

"Cass!" Shenice said urgently, grabbing my arm.

Her gaze slid to the front of my blouse and she raised her eyebrows as though trying to tell me something. Again, I ignored her. Seriously, did she think I didn't KNOW there was a great greasy stain floating in its lake of water on the front of my blouse?

Then I realized what Shen was getting at. Seeping through the sodden cotton of my blouse was a small but perfectly formed picture of a cutesy little FAIRY. I dabbed at the mess carefully, hoping Nathan might not notice. I was beginning to wonder whether the universe had it in for me; it had certainly done its best to out me as a former FAIRY FANGIRL. I was only wearing the stupid vest because Mum had insisted.

"So it's been great chatting and all but I really need to go now," I gabbled, covering the fairy's smile with my arm and backing away. "See you later."

"Wait!" he called but I scurried away to safety. That had been too close. The moment I got home, this fairy was HISTORY.

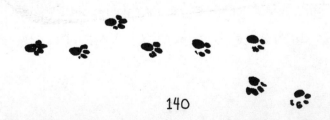

St Jude's Academy
Churchbell Avenue, Windsor, SL4 8QP

Dear Mr and Mrs Bond,

I am writing to invite you to attend a meeting with me this Wednesday at 3.35 p.m. to discuss Cassidy's ongoing education.

The matter is quite urgent so if this day and time are not convenient for you, please contact the school to rearrange as soon as possible.

Many thanks,

Mr P Archer

Head of Year Seven

???

CHAPTER FOURTEEN

We've been back two days after the half-term holiday and ALREADY my parents have been summoned to ANOTHER meeting with Mr Archer. I haven't got a clue what it's about, unless it's something to do with the Molly situation, but why would Mr Archer be involved with that? Shenice reckons I've been nominated for a brainy person's award or something. I suppose she might be right but I don't think I've done anything to deserve one. I mean, I did manage to make my copper sulphate turn blue in science once but I don't think they give the Nobel Prize for that,

do they? Especially not when everyone else in the class did
it as well.

I'm amazed he's prepared to have Mum back in his office
after last time, to be honest. She's even bigger now and I'm
pretty sure the ground SHAKES when she walks. But I
suppose he doesn't have much choice. I hope they don't make
a habit of these meetings – apart from anything else, Liam
has started calling me TEACHER'S PET. He's just jealous
because his meetings with the school always involve the
words "final warning".

At least being in the meeting means I won't have
to see Molly walking home on her own. A little sliver
of sympathy sneaked through my wall of anger yesterday
and I tried texting her again but she ignored it. Seriously,
she's the most stubborn person I know – she is trying
not to show it but I bet she's lonely. I wish she would
get over her pride and be friends again. It's HORRIBLE
being enemies.

I cannot believe this is happening. The meeting with Mr Archer wasn't about a special award or anything even half as good. It turns out that there was a mix-up with the CAT papers and my result was swapped with the OTHER C Bond. So she's the SUPER-GENIUS and I'm back to being MISS AVERAGE. Her name is Clarissa, apparently, which is even worse than mine. I might feel sorry for her if she hadn't stolen the only thing I've ever felt proud of. Mr Archer was very apologetic and says nothing like it has ever happened before. He's spoken to my teachers, who have agreed that I can stay on the GIFTED AND TALENTED register until the end of the term, to make it less obvious I am not a SUPER-GENIUS after all, but who cares about that? The worst thing is that I'd have been happy with my real results before I thought I was clever. Now I just feel stupid.

At least I don't have to worry about quitting the quiz team any more – I expect Mr Bearman will have already replaced me with Clarissa. So I don't have to tell Nathan, which is a bonus.

Mum and Dad tried to cheer me up by saying that BRAINS aren't everything, which was nice of them but didn't exactly help. Who are they kidding, anyway? I've been smart and I've been ordinary and I know which one I preferred. And Liam is going to make all kinds of jokes. Oh God. Rebecca is going to be so smug.

Why couldn't this have happened before I spent all those hours researching freaky facts?

To: BondGirl007
From: Membership@CleverClogs

Dear Miss Bond,
Thank you for your email about joining Clever Clogs. I am sorry to hear about the unfortunate mix-up at school, although I think the phrase "identity theft" may be a little strong.

As you may already know, Clever Clogs is a high IQ society which accepts membership from anyone with an IQ in the top two per cent of the population. We would be happy to welcome you as a member if you are able to prove your IQ meets our requirements. However, I am afraid our current rules do not allow me to accept a *Glitz* magazine crossword puzzle as evidence of intelligence, even if it is completed.

There is a home test you can do if you would like to get an idea of your intelligence level and I would be happy to send a copy to you. In answer to your query, I do not think there are any questions about cats.
Kind regards,
Bharti Ahmed
Clever Clogs Membership Assistant

CHAPTER FIFTEEN

The shambles that is my existence continues. I didn't even try to convince Mum I was ill this morning, that's how depressed I am. The irony is that it might actually have worked; she knows I normally like Thursdays (double English – YAY!) and seemed concerned about me for once – she even tried to feel my forehead but I batted her hand away. What's the point of avoiding school today when I'll have to go TOMORROW and NEXT WEEK and the WEEK AFTER THAT?

Mr Bearman actually tried to convince me to stay on the quiz team. He said lots of nice things about EMOTIONAL INTELLIGENCE and how I have something UNIQUE to offer the team, but really I think he has realized there are only four days to go until the team's first test at the regional heats and that a LAME DUCK is better than no duck at all. Presumably Clarissa Bond is above such petty things as TEAM ST JUDE'S and declined their offer of a place on the team. It wasn't hard to ignore Mr Bearman's reasoning though; I just pictured myself getting question after question wrong and that was enough to ensure I didn't get sucked into staying on the team.

"I can't say I'm not disappointed, Cassie," Mr Bearman said, when it became obvious I wasn't going to change my mind. "I think you made a real difference to the team."

"Yeah, the difference between winning and losing,"
I replied morosely. "And just in case there's any confusion,
I doubt any of the team thinks I'd help them win. Ask
Rebecca if you don't believe me."

He sighed. "Isn't there anything I can do to persuade
you?"

Short of turning back the clock to yesterday, there
wasn't. "No, sir."

Spreading his hands, he looked genuinely disappointed.
"We'll have to manage without you, then. Let's hope there
aren't any Harry Potter questions, eh?"

Reasons I Hate Life

Stupid Molly.

Stupid Liam teasing me.

Stupid school mixing up the tests and making me think I was somehow special.

Stupid Mum complaining about stupid back pain ALL THE TIME.

Stupid neighbours complaining about Rolo chasing their cat. It serves them right for having a stupid cat.

Stupid fairies.

STUPID EVERYTHING.

Dad has decided that the best thing he can do to cheer me up is sing Elvis at me. It would be a lot more uplifting if he didn't seem to have "HEARTBREAK HOTEL" on loop, though. He says I used to love it when I was a baby. I am not sure if he has noticed but I am not a baby any more and the lyrics are super depressing.

Liam's reaction has been typically gloating. First, he boasts about having more friends than me (I assume he means that he has taken Molly away from me, which I suppose is true but it isn't the sort of thing I'd mention too much if I was a fourteen-year-old boy) and then he says that because he beat me at Trivial Pursuit last Christmas, he is clearly the BRAINS of the family as well as the TALENT. I wouldn't mind but he only won because he CHEATED and sneaked an extra wedge in when he thought we weren't looking – believe me, no one has ever accused him of being intelligent. As for talent – ha, he's not even that good at the guitar. And I have a higher score than him on GUITAR HERO. One of these days I might remind him of that.

"Have you got a minute, Cassie?"

Nathan didn't smile. He stood in front of my table
as the bell rang at the end of English, signalling the very
welcome end of Friday's lessons. Would he be offended if
I leaped over the desk to avoid him? Shenice pulled a
sympathetic face but we both knew there was no escaping
this showdown.

"Sure," I replied, trying to sound casual. "What can I
do for you?"

"Not here," he said. "I thought maybe I could – uh –
walk you home or something."

On the next table, I could see Molly straining to
overhear what was going on as she packed her bag;
if she'd been any more obvious, her ears would have

WAGGLED. Mr Bearman wasn't winning any prizes for subtlety at the front of the class, either; he kept glancing over and I guessed he'd asked Nathan to have a little chat with me.

I let out a heavy sigh. "Okay. See you tomorrow, Shen."

She got the message and nodded, making a "CALL ME" sign with her fingers before heading out of the class. Nathan waited until I'd packed up my stuff, which I did as slowly as possible, purely to see what Molly did. She was clearly DYING of CURIOSITY because she slowed down too, but eventually there was nothing left on the table in front of her and she had to admit defeat and leave. I knew she'd be dawdling in front of us all the way home, hoping to work out what was going on.

Nathan didn't waste any time in getting to the point as we left the school grounds.

"Mr Bearman says you've dropped out of the quiz team."

I pulled my scarf up around my mouth and tried not to mind that my legs had turned to ice. Seriously, WHY are girls at St Jude's not allowed to wear trousers? Ahead, I could see Molly and I slowed down a little. "Yeah. I'm sorry but I just can't do it."

"But why? I thought you were great," said Nathan.

I rolled my eyes. "Mr Bearman put you up to this, didn't he?"

Nathan shrugged. "We've got a massive hole in our team knowledge. Rebecca and Bilal are all right at the academic questions but they're rubbish on stuff like chart

music and TV and it's let us down before." He turned
to me. "That's where you come in."

I blinked. "What do you mean?"

"Molly told me that you're the QUEEN
of POP CULTURE," he said, grinning.
"She said that what you don't know
about boy bands isn't worth knowing."

For a minute I was confused, then I remembered
Nathan and Molly were old friends and the penny dropped
– suddenly all that stuff Mr Bearman had said about my
unique contribution to the team made sense. "So I wasn't
recruited because of my CAT score?"

"Nope," he said, throwing me a curious look. "Why,
was it good?"

The fact that he hadn't even known about the stupid

CATs changed everything, and I didn't feel so stupid. "So you haven't asked Clarissa Bond to take my place?"

He looked interested. "Not yet. Why, does she know more about THE DROIDS than you?"

I snorted. "I doubt it. No one knows more about them than me."

We reached the front garden of my house. Nathan stopped. "Then you're the only Bond for the job. What do you reckon? Fancy kicking some Royal Windsor butt next week?"

Pretending to think about it, I stared at Molly a few houses away, touched that she'd talked me up to Nathan. Then again, it was typical Molly — at primary school, she always looked out for Shen and me. It reminded me what a great friend she was, and how much I miss her. Maybe I should try harder to make things right. "Go on, then."

"Good," Nathan said, sounding satisfied. "Because I'm not sure Rebecca would recognize ZIGGY and RORY if they passed her on the street."

I grinned and pushed open the gate. "Right." There was a yowl and a volley of barks from around the back of the house. I winced. "I'd better go in. That sounds like Rolo and who knows what he's destroying this time."

Nathan laughed, but in a sympathetic way. "No worries."

With a wave, he headed off down the street. I had a little grin to myself as I went in to see what my dog was up to now. I was back on the team, and this time, it felt like I belonged there. Suddenly, things were looking up.

To: BondGirl007
From: NPellow

Dear Miss Bond,

Thanks for your enquiry about taking part in Junior Mastermind. At present, there are no plans for a new series of the quiz but we will keep your details on file in case this changes. I can confirm that specialist subjects of The Droids or SpongeBob SquarePants would both be equally acceptable. "The Many Flavours of Quality Street" would not.

Yours sincerely,

N Pellow

BBC Light Entertainment

CHAPTER SIXTEEN

Monday again, but this one could not be more different to last week. On top of some heavy duty hard work for the quiz next week, preparations for ST JUDE'S HAS GOT TALENT are starting properly now. With only three weeks until the live acts perform in an afternoon show, the judging panel has set up auditions and they're screening the performers so that only the best go through. Part of me hopes WOLF BRETHREN are weeded out early on – that will shut Liam right up and stop him from gloating quite so much. I'm actually glad I didn't enter in the end

– performing looks **TERRIFYING**. I have everything crossed that Molly's audition goes okay. After what she did for me with Nathan, without giving me the tiniest clue she was doing it, I feel like the least I can do is root for her. I've also decided that once the quiz team regionals are out of the way today, me and Shenice are going to sort this argument out. Even if one of us has to sit on Molly to make her listen.

Speaking of the regionals, I'm getting more and more nervous about them. I spent the whole weekend revising but it's hard to know what to study. I slipped Mum's **JANE EYRE** DVD into my Harry Potter marathon, in case there are any questions on the classics, but it didn't half drag on. What it needs is a few **ZOMBIES** – they would have spiced things up no end. Anyway, I'm starting to feel glad that I'm not a **SUPER-GENIUS** after all – it sounds like there'd be a lot of this kind of thing involved and I'm not sure I'm really cut out for intensive studying.

Rebecca and Bilal seemed pleased to see me when I turned up to get on the school minibus to go to ROYAL WINDSOR PREPARATORY SCHOOL that afternoon.
I suppose it made sense;
without me, they'd have
been one player short
against the other teams.

By the time we'd arrived, I was starting to feel sick with nerves. Nathan looked like he had ICE for BLOOD, he was so CHILLED OUT, and the others hardly looked worried either. They'd all done this before, though; I was the only newbie. I suppose it would be weirder if I wasn't nervous.

We were led into a large wood-panelled hall filled with tables, where lots of other teams were already sitting. Noisy chatter filled the air and on the wall was a huge, unsmiling picture of the Queen. At the front of the hall, there was a giant screen, which almost made me pine for popcorn. Almost. Mr Bearman found our table and we settled into our seats. He checked his watch.

"They'll be starting soon," he said, patting Nathan on the shoulder. Then he nodded towards the chairs around the edge of the hall. "I'll be sitting over there with the other teachers. Good luck, Team SJ!"

"There's the Royal Windsor lot," Nathan said, pointing to a group of kids in burgundy blazers a few tables away. "They beat us every time we competed against them at our old school."

I crossed my fingers and hoped his faith in me wasn't a mistake, as I watched a man dressed in a multi-coloured waistcoat and carrying a microphone walk into the hall.

"Welcome to the regional heat of this year's KIDS' QUIZ!" he exclaimed. "My name is Winston Jacobs.

Are you ready to have your brains TEASED and your memories TESTED?"

Every table cheered in reply.

"Then let's get started!" he said. "Don't forget to make sure those phones are off. Anyone caught using one will be immediately expelled from the hall, and that goes for you teachers too!"

The room was filled with rustling as a hundred phones were switched off. Winston nodded in satisfaction. "Excellent. Now, pens at the ready and brain cells steady, here we go with Round One – IT'S SO NATURAL."

One by one, he read out the questions, which were all about natural history. After each one, fierce whispering broke out on every table. Rebecca was in charge of writing our answers onto our sheet and, boy, did she take it seriously. Her tongue stuck out when she wrote and she was frowning so hard it had to hurt.

Nathan spotted my raised eyebrows. "If the quiz markers can't read our answers, they won't give us the points," he murmured. "We lost the junior title because of it once."

Which made Rebecca's concentration easier to understand. This was Bilal's specialist round so I didn't have to provide any answers but I was surprised to realize I did know some of them. Maybe all that studying had done me some good.

Our answer sheets were collected and Winston started on Round Two, which was all about sport. I didn't know a single answer and wished I could phone a friend; Shenice is FOOTBALL CRAZY and would definitely know which team won the FA Cup in 2008. As it was, Nathan was pretty hot on sport so we did okay.

Round after round went by. The scores were displayed on the screen and it soon became clear that a few schools were streaking out in front. It was us versus Royal Windsor! I caught one of the girls glaring at us and smiled sweetly back. As the rounds ticked by, the room was filled with the sound of hushed conversations and feverish scribbling. Although Nathan did his best to include me, and I did supply a few answers, I didn't really feel needed until Winston announced the penultimate round.

"Here's one to test your knowledge of all things trivial," he called. "POP GOES THE WEASEL is the perfect round for anyone who keeps up with the gossip columns."

I resisted the urge to punch the air. "Yes!" I hissed, grinning at the others. "This is my kind of round."

It was as though someone had looked into my head and plucked out the PERFECT set of questions for me. Which celeb recently named their baby daughter Honey

Cheeks? Which artist sold the most copies of their album last year? Who refused to present the Best Actress Oscar unless they were promised a Tiffany's goody bag for their Chihuahua? ⟶

At the end of the round, I knew I'd nailed all ten questions. Beaming, I caught Nathan's eye.

"Royal Windsor don't look quite as comfortable as they did," he said, grinning back at me. "Nice work, Cassie."

I held my breath as the scores were updated. We'd been neck and neck with the hosts all the way through but had dropped two points in the last round and Royal Windsor had edged in front. As I'd hoped, we'd got every pop culture question right. If Royal Windsor couldn't match us then we stood a chance of taking the lead.

"It's tight at the top," Winston declared, as the screen flickered and refreshed. "But thanks to a storming performance in that last round, St Jude's have caught up and are tied with Royal Windsor for first place!"

I couldn't help it; I let out a loud SQUEAK of EXCITEMENT. It was all down to the final round – literature. A sudden wave of anxiety sloshed away my earlier euphoria at our perfect score; Royal Windsor looked like a bunch of bookworms. They were bound to do well in this round. The question was, could we keep up?

We were doing well up to the last question. Then the thing I'd been dreading happened; a difference of opinion between me and Rebecca.

"Question ten: In the correct order, list the full name of Professor Dumbledore, the Headmaster of Hogwarts

School." Winston peered around the room, a serious expression on his face. "And as the scores are so close, we will need the order to be exactly right to award the point."

Without a word, Rebecca bent her head and began to scribble down the answer.

"Hang on," I protested. "Aren't you going to ask us?"

She didn't look up. "No, I know the answer."

I craned my head, trying to read what she was writing. "So do I. And you've got it wrong — it's Albus Percival Wulfric Brian Dumbledore. You've put Brian in the wrong place."

Rebecca lowered her pen. "No, Professor Dumbledore's full name is Albus Percival Brian Wulfric, in that order."

Folding my arms, I met her stare. "Want to bet?"

Nathan looked from Rebecca to me. "They're collecting the answers in. We need to decide now."

"I promise you, I'm right," I insisted, willing him to trust me.

He hesitated. "Okay, let's put it to the vote. Who thinks it's Percival Brian?"

Predictably, Bilal and Rebecca raised their hands.

"Which means me and Cassie think Wulfric comes after Percival." Nathan thought for a moment, then closed his eyes. "I hope you're right, Cassie. Put Albus Percival Wulfric Brian."

I thought for a second Rebecca was going to refuse but then she picked up her pen and changed it. Before any of us could speak, the paper was snatched from the table and taken to the markers.

Instantly, my stomach started to roll. What if I was wrong? Had I just lost us the quiz? One look at the faces of my team-mates told me they were wondering the same thing.

It felt like **FOR EVER** until all the scores had been updated. The screen didn't change, though. Instead, Winston stood up and held his hands out for quiet.

"Now, the moment you've all been waiting for – the results! It's been a real nail-biter but in third place, we have Riverside Secondary School with eighty-eight points!"

Applause broke out and Riverside let out a volley of loud whoops.

Winston waited for the noise to die down. "In second place, with a brilliant ninety-one points, is…" He paused in a way that made me think he'd been watching way too much X FACTOR and gazed around. "Royal Windsor Preparatory School!"

We'd done it – WE'D WON! All four of us leaped to our feet, yelling and cheering. I glanced over at Royal Windsor to see them politely clapping. They looked like they'd lost a winning lottery ticket.

"And the winners of today's regional heat, with an amazing ninety-two points out of one hundred, is St Jude's Secondary School!" Winston finished. "Congratulations, Team SJ!"

Mr Bearman headed our way, smiling proudly. Rebecca looked like she was going to cry and Bilal had the biggest smile plastered across his face.

"You know what this means?" Nathan said, grinning at me. "We got full marks in that last round. You were right."

"Never doubted it," I lied.

Then he leaned towards me and I thought for one heart-stopping second he was going to hug me. But he let his arms drop at the last moment. "See? I knew you were going to be our secret weapon."

What can I say? I might not be the brightest student in our year but I'd come through when it mattered. And believe me, it felt good. Really, really good.

Cassie's Extremely Secret Diary

To-Do List

1. Win Kids' Quiz – DONE!

2. Make up with Molly – I don't even care who apologizes to who now, I just want our fight to be OVER.

3. Train Rolo to be a good dog, one who does not disappear when let off the lead so that the police have to bring him home.

4. Work out if Nathan likes me – this is so hard. I mean, sometimes I think he does but how can I be sure? How does anyone EVER get together?

5. Become more self-sufficient, so that when the babies come, I can look after myself – DONE. I can now cook cheese on toast AND beans on toast.

6. Be staggeringly famous – DONE. Yay me!

CHAPTER SEVENTEEN

The thing about doing something amazing, like winning the regional heat of the Kids' Quiz for the first time in the history of your school for example, is that news travels pretty fast. Especially when the Headteacher speeds things along by getting all emotional about it in assembly. So for a whole week after Team SJ had brought home the glory, the four of us were heroes. Okay, so the older year groups were less impressed, and some of them thought we were **TOTAL GEEKS**, but the rest of Year Seven thought we were **AWESOME**. I wondered what

would happen if we won the national quiz next term —
we'd be total legends. Well, Rebecca, Bilal and me would be.
Nathan already is. Did I mention how much I LIKE him?

But then the buzz about winning the quiz faded and
ST JUDE'S HAS GOT TALENT fever took hold. Seriously,
it's like Willy Wonka has released another batch of Golden
Tickets and you can only get one by embarrassing yourself
in front of the judges. People I'd never have suspected of
wanting their fifteen minutes of fame have suddenly come
out with dubious talents of all descriptions and the entire
playground seems to have turned into a rehearsal space.
Is ARMPIT FARTING the national anthem really a skill?
Anyway, I am starting to have more respect for Liam and
the other members of WOLF BRETHREN; next to some of
the acts, they do look like rock gods.

The auditions are going on all this week, with the
finalists being announced on 28th November. That means
I have another seven more days of Liam's strops to put up

with – seriously, he is dealing with the stress of waiting by competing with Mum in the moodiness stakes. And it will only get worse if WOLF BRETHREN reach the finals. I may start going with Dad to his Elvis gigs just to get away from the atmosphere at home, and if that doesn't paint you a picture of how DESPERATE I am, nothing will.

It feels to me like Mum has been pregnant for ever. Her bump is so large that it is in danger of altering the sun's gravitational field and I fully expect NASA to announce that all the planets have mysteriously begun to orbit the Earth. She's really struggling to move around now and it won't be long before she can't fit behind the wheel of the car any more. I feel bad watching her waddle around and am trying not to let her grumpiness get to me; if my stomach was the size of an over-inflated SPACE HOPPER, I might be stroppy too. She's got this thing called carpal tunnel syndrome in her hands as well, which means she can't open the jars of pickled onions to have with her bananas.

Overall, I think that's probably a good thing, though.
I hope the twins appreciate what she is going through
for them; I'm sure I was never this much trouble.

I still haven't had a chance to make up with Molly.
Shenice agrees that she did a nice thing in talking me up to
Nathan, and that she must have done it on the quiet before
we fell out, but she hasn't got a clue about how to fix our
broken friendship. It doesn't help that Molly is still **WOLF
BRETHREN**'s number one groupie. Maybe things will get
easier once **SJHGT** is over and we can all be friends again.
I hope so. Shen's great but it's not the same without Molly.
We're like **SNAP** and **CRACKLE** without **POP**.

The list of finalists is up on the school website and –
OMG TO THE MAX – Molly's name is there! So is **WOLF
BRETHREN**'s but I kind of expected that. I know I go on
about Liam being rubbish at guitar but I suppose they
are pretty good at their own kind of **THRASH-TASTIC**

rock, if you like that sort of thing.

I can't believe Molly is going to have to sing in front of the whole school. She talked about auditioning but I wasn't sure she'd really go through with it. Nathan says she admitted to him that she's really nervous about performing in front of everybody, which made me wonder if she's talked to him about why we fell out — probably not. It would have made stuff really awkward for him. Anyway, it didn't surprise me to hear she's worried about her performance but, knowing Molly, I reckon she'll be desperate to show everyone what she's made of, too. I wish I could tell her how pleased I am for her. I have settled for asking the universe to help her to win.

I'm so glad that the ARMPIT FARTER didn't make the final cut. Tickets are only two pounds fifty but there are some things I'd pay NOT to see. There are three dance acts, four singers, Liam's band and something else called REPERCUSSION — whatever that is. Oh, and someone's dog has made it into the final – I'm not even kidding. I might have thought about entering with Rolo if I'd known dogs were allowed on the premises. Although thinking about it, probably not. He'd try to eat everyone's lunch or something.

With only a week until the final, the hype around school is unbelievable. Seriously, Simon Cowell could learn a thing or two from St Jude's about whipping people into a FRENZY. Everyone is talking about who their favourite act is and rivalries are breaking out between fans. Even Molly has stopped handing out WOLF BRETHREN flyers at lunchtime. I know who I'll be voting for. Blood might be thicker than water but you can't just ignore seven years of friendship, even though we've hit a bump right now. She's been there for me in the past; the least I can do now is support her, whether she wants me to or not.

I am really glad I decided not to enter SJHGT. Liam is so tired from all the extra rehearsals WOLF BRETHREN have been putting in that he can hardly string a sentence together. Some people (i.e. me) might say that's a good thing but I think Dad is worried Liam is going to **PASS OUT** onstage during the final today. He tried to give him a pep talk over breakfast this morning – Liam just grunted like a **ZOMBIE** and crunched his toast. At least it's the weekend tomorrow and the contest will be over – I suppose he can sleep all day if he wants to, and we can all chill out a bit. Except for Mum, who can't get comfy anywhere and looks like she is about to pop.

The school theatre has been off limits for the last two days so that it can be decorated. There are rumours that the drama department has built three gigantic light-up Xs above the judges' seats and that our Deputy Head, Mrs Pitt-Rivers, will be **TWERKING** while the votes are being counted. I have no idea whether either of these rumours is true but I'm pretty sure no one wants to see Mrs Pitt-Rivers SHAKE HER THANG.

The excitement in the air was
almost at fever pitch by the time
we all filed into the theatre and sat
down. There was a massive ST JUDE'S HAS
GOT TALENT banner above the stage,
surrounded by red, white and blue balloons, and
there were two giant screens on either side of it. On each
seat, there was a ballot sheet. I exchanged an excited look
with Shenice; at some point in the next ninety minutes,
Molly might be taking home the ST JUDE'S HAS GOT
TALENT trophy. She'd be the nearest thing the school had
to a celeb!

Mrs Pitt-Rivers climbed up the steps to the stage and
waited for the chatter to die down. Muffled giggling broke
out and I guessed people were wondering if the rumours
were true. I doubted it – surely she couldn't be planning to
DANCE in that long tweed skirt and bobbly cardigan?

"Welcome to the first ever ST JUDE'S HAS GOT

TALENT!" she said, and there was a screech of feedback from the microphone. "We have some amazing acts lined up for you this afternoon but first, please welcome our judges!"

We clapped as the music from THE APPRENTICE boomed out of the speakers and the three judges – the Head of Year Ten, Mr Bearman and the Headteacher – took their seats in front of the stage.

Mrs Pitt-Rivers raised her microphone again. "Here's how the contest will work. Each act will perform once. You will get the chance to vote for your favourite. Then the judges will choose the overall winner out of the three most popular acts."

The white screens to either side of the stage burst into life and the names of the acts appeared in what I supposed was the running order. I nudged Shenice; Molly was on fourth, after POM-POM THE PERFORMING POODLE.

WOLF BRETHREN were on second to last, after TRUE STREET CREW but before REPERCUSSION.

"And now, please welcome our first performers – TWO 2 TANGO!"

Leading the applause, Mrs Pitt-Rivers backed off stage and a boy and a girl I vaguely recognized from Year Ten came on. The girl wore a slinky black and red dress, split all the way up her thigh, and her partner had a matching red shirt and black trousers. I knew they were going to be good before they'd even danced a step.

And they were; they looked like they'd fit right in with the pros on STRICTLY COME DANCING. The next act was a Year-Eight boy, who sang "BABY" by Justin Bieber – he wasn't half-bad either. Both of the acts so far had been great and I started to feel really nervous for Molly. It had been a while since I'd heard her sing – was she good enough to beat all these brilliant performers?

The standard was so high. Then POM-POM THE POODLE and her owner took to the stage and things went a bit wrong. I won't go into detail but let's just say they quite literally put the poo into "poodle".

It took several long minutes to clear up after Pom-Pom and my quivering nerves got worse. Beside me, I could see Shenice nibbling at her nails as Molly walked onstage. We needn't have worried, though – she was unbelievably AWESOME. She stood there like she was born to perform and sang "You Raise Me Up", by some American guy called Josh Groban. Her voice was note-perfect and beautiful and the whole theatre was transfixed. I swear I even saw Mrs Pitt-Rivers wiping away a tear at the end and the applause was thundering.

Next up was another dance act, followed by a girl singer who was nowhere near as good as Molly and a boy who forgot his words. Then TRUE STREET CREW came on and their routine was packed with sharp moves.

I recognized a couple of Year-Seven kids in the squad – on another day, they might have got my vote.

About halfway through their performance, I felt my phone vibrate in my pocket. I pulled it out to see a text from Liam. *Meet me in the corridor. NOW.*

I frowned at the screen. What was he doing texting me? Wasn't he about to go onstage?

Why? I replied, trying not to let any teachers see me do it. The last thing I needed was to have my phone confiscated on a Friday afternoon.

Less than ten seconds went by before my phone vibrated again. *Just do it!*

Scowling, I looked along my row of seats. I'd have to get everyone to stand up to let me pass; people would complain. Whatever Liam wanted, it would have to wait.

My pocket buzzed insistently. *Hurry up! It's important.*

I let out a sigh and leaned towards Shenice. "I've got to go. BRB."

Puzzled, she half stood and I squeezed past her. Tuts and muttering broke out as I made my way along the row of seats. Then I was in the aisle and heading for the exit.

One of the teachers stopped me. "Where are you going?"

"Toilet, sir," I whispered. Seeing he was about to send me back to my seat, I improvised a bit more. "I think I might have that tummy bug that's been going around. The really sicky one."

I've never seen anyone back off so fast and I guessed he had plans for the weekend.

"Come straight back here when you've finished," he said, not quite managing to stop his hand from covering his mouth. "Be as quick as you can."

I nodded and slipped out into the corridor. The door to the theatre closed behind me, muting TRUE STREET CREW's music and I looked around for Liam. He was hovering at the end of the corridor, by the doors to the dressing rooms. I frowned; was he really dressed as a werewolf?

"Liam!" I stage-whispered. "What do you want?"

He turned and saw me. As he hurried forwards, I realized his expression wasn't that of a nervous performer; he was worried.

"I've just had a text from Dad," he said, his voice tight. "Mum's been rushed to hospital. We need to go, right now."

187

CHAPTER EIGHTEEN

My stomach twisted at Liam's words and suddenly the SICK FEELING I'd invented to get out of the theatre seemed all too real. The babies weren't due until Boxing Day — if they were on their way now, they'd be more than three weeks early. That couldn't be a good thing.

"What happened?" I demanded. "Is something wrong with them?"

He shook his head. "I don't think so. Dad said Mum's

waters broke and the hospital told them to get there as fast as they could. Auntie Jane is coming to pick us up."

I stared at his white face and forced myself to breathe slowly. "So he didn't say there was a problem? Just that they shouldn't waste any time going to the hospital?"

Liam checked his phone. "Yeah. I've told the lads I can't go onstage with them. They understand."

I leaned forwards and read the text message from Dad. There was no mention of any real danger and it actually sounded as though everything was under control. My stomach muscles started to unclench and I began to relax. The hospital was probably being cautious; surely they tell every pregnant woman to go in once her waters break, let alone the ones having twins. It would probably be ages yet. Like I said, I've seen **ONE BORN EVERY MINUTE** and sometimes it takes days. Then Liam's final comment filtered through to my brain. "You're not going onstage? Why not?"

He ran an agitated hand through his over-waxed hair. "I can't. We need to get to the hospital."

Applause broke out in the theatre; TRUE STREET CREW must have finished their performance.

I shook my head at Liam. "You should go on with the band," I told him, amazed at how much calmer than him I was. "It'll take Auntie Jane a while to get here from across town and ten more minutes isn't going to make any difference."

He threw a longing backwards glance at the stage door. "You think so? Mum and Dad won't mind?"

"I think they'll have other things on their plates right now," I said, pulling a face. "They've probably forgotten we even exist. In fact, we should get used to that."

He still hesitated and I shooed him towards the stage doors.

"Look, I'll text Dad and make sure everything is okay. Now go, or you'll miss your big moment."

Flashing me a grateful look, he turned and ran to the stage doors. I fired off a quick text to Dad, and one to Auntie Jane, then hurried back into the theatre. Seconds later, WOLF BRETHREN appeared on the stage in their weird werewolf outfits, and wild clapping broke out. I picked my way back to my seat, impressed at the cheers. Obviously, WOLF BRETHREN were more popular than I'd realized.

Once they started playing, I understood why – they were REALLY good. Liam's guitar playing had improved with all the extra practice and the lead singer didn't shout half as much as the last time I'd heard them play. Maybe Liam's dream of being a rock star isn't as mental as I'd thought.

Shenice looked as surprised as me that they didn't suck. She pulled this **AMAZED** face as I sat down. I didn't tell her what I'd been doing; I'd wait for an update from Dad before I explained.

WOLF BRETHREN finished in a flurry of drums and wailing guitars. Around me, people got to their feet and cheered. I chewed my lip anxiously — the overall winner was going to be a tough one to call. Suddenly, I wasn't sure Molly had it in the bag after all.

The final act, **REPERCUSSION**, came onto the stage. There were about ten of them, mostly from Years Ten and Eleven. They had no instruments but some carried tin cans, others had a couple of long thick

sticks and a few had brooms. No one in the audience seemed to know what to expect. Then Shenice gasped.

"I know what this is!" she whispered to me. "My dad took me to see this show in London called STOMP. Basically, they sort of drum, using everyday objects. I bet that's what REPERCUSSION are going to do."

I grimaced – it sounded like a terrible idea. But then they started to play, softly at first with a tip-tapping rhythm brushed out on the floor with the bristles of the brooms. Gradually, it built up with more and more sounds from the unlikeliest of instruments – who knew a fast-food carton could carry a tune? Soon, the whole theatre was rocking to the beat of the tin cans, bottles and sticks. The brooms were replaced by steel drums and the movement was so fast it was hypnotic. I watched, mesmerized, and even forgot about Mum and Dad and the babies for a few minutes. By the time REPERCUSSION reached a crescendo, it sounded as if every single person in the theatre was tapping their feet to the beat. As the final crash of drums died away, there was a moment's awed silence and then we all went crazy. I had no idea brushes and cans could sound so cool!

The applause lasted for AGES but I was too busy checking my phone for a text from Dad or Auntie Jane to clap for long. My stomach TWISTED again as I saw the blank screen — no news had to be good news, right? As the noise started to die down, Mrs Pitt-Rivers came back onstage and told us it was decision time. All around me, people started to pick up their voting slips. I stared down at mine and tried to push my concern to one side. Half an hour earlier, I'd been sure who had my vote but now? My pen hovered over WOLF BRETHREN for a second — they had totally smashed it and Liam WAS my brother after all, even if I usually tried to pretend he wasn't. And for a minute back then, when he'd been worried about Mum and the twins, he'd almost seemed human. But Molly had been amazing too and we'd been friends for ever. Well, apart from the last six weeks, obviously, but that didn't matter any more. Making up my mind, I placed a big tick next to her name and looked over at Shenice in time to see her do the same. Molly might not be everyone else's choice but she was definitely a WINNER to us.

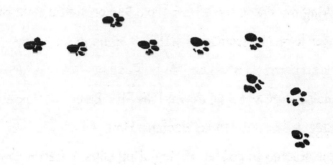

CHAPTER NINETEEN

"Well, I'm sure you'll all agree that St Jude's has a lot of very talented students!"

After a lifetime of waiting, during which I checked for messages so often that my phone grew hot, Mrs Pitt-Rivers was back onstage and ten nervous-looking acts were lined up behind her. A sheen of sweat glistened on Liam's forehead and Molly looked like she might vom at any moment. Sneaking another quick peek at my phone, I decided I knew how she felt.

"The votes have been counted and the judges have deliberated," the Deputy Head went on. "Now it's time to announce the winner of ST JUDE'S HAS GOT TALENT!"

I held my breath and crossed my fingers. Would it be Molly? Or had one of the other acts beaten her to it?

Holding up a sheet of paper, Mrs Pitt-Rivers cleared her throat. "In third place...MOLLY PAPADOPOULOS!"

I let out a loud whoop and clapped so hard my hands stung. Beside me, Shenice stamped her feet in appreciation. Molly looked genuinely delighted and waved at the cheering audience.

"In second place...WOLF BRETHREN!"

I felt a momentary burst of automatic INDIGNATION – Molly had been way better than the band – before I remembered that WOLF BRETHREN had been good and

I cheered along with the rest of the crowd. But if Liam was second and Molly was third, who had come first?

"And in first place, after a breathtaking performance...REPERCUSSION!"

The applause was so loud I thought my eardrums might burst. REPERCUSSION stepped forwards to accept the trophy and the cheque from the smiling Headteacher. Shenice looked at me with a shrug. Neither of us could deny that REPERCUSSION had been brilliant and probably deserved to win. But I could tell we both wished Molly had taken first place.

As REPERCUSSION smiled and lifted their prize, my phone vibrated in my pocket. Hardly daring to breathe, I read the text message.

Twins have landed! Get here as soon as you can! Love, Dad x

My heart swelled until I thought it might pop. Reaching across to Shenice, I flung my arms around her. She stared at me, shocked.

"Er...okay. What's going on?"

I showed her my phone and an enormous grin crossed her face. "CONGRATULATIONS!"

"Thanks!" I replied, and the word came out as an excited squeak. "I can't believe I'm a big sister at last!"

Looking at the stage, I caught Liam scanning the crowd for me and gave him a big thumbs up. Grinning, he returned the gesture. As the acts stood around congratulating each other, the bell rang to signal the end of the school day and everyone got ready to leave the theatre. My phone buzzed again. This time, it was Auntie Jane. *Stuck in traffic! Be there ASAP xx*

Swinging my bag onto my shoulder, I squeezed past Shenice again. "I'd better go, my aunt is on her way. I'll send you a pic as soon as I have one."

She nodded. "Give them a kiss from their Auntie Shenice."

I was halfway down the stairs when I heard someone call my name. Turning, I saw it was Nathan. I stopped and waited for him to reach me.

"Shame about Molly," he said. "But REPERCUSSION were good, I suppose."

"Yeah, they were. And Molly looks happy with her third place." I smiled. "At least she beat the poodle."

"True." He coughed and cleared his throat. If I hadn't known better, I'd have said he was nervous. "I wondered if you were around this weekend? I thought we could do

200

some quiz cramming together or something."

My mouth fell open. I closed it fast. Was he asking me out? Or did he mean a full Team SJ cramming session? Then I remembered that it didn't matter much, either way; I wasn't free.

"Actually, I'm just on my way to the hospital," I explained. "My mum has had the twins."

His face lit up. "Really? How cool – congratulations!"

How to handle my reply so that I didn't look like an idiot if he'd meant a group meeting? I pondered. "But I'm definitely free over the Christmas holidays."

He grinned. "Good to know."

I smiled back and we stood grinning at each other for ages, until Nathan blinked and said, "Uh – hadn't you better get going?"

OMG, he was RIGHT. But there was something I had to do first.

Molly saw me coming but before she could say a word, I held out my hand. In it was a WHAM BAR.

"Truce?" I asked, trying to keep my voice from wobbling.

I thought for a moment she was going to refuse it but then she took the sweet and nodded. Before she could change her mind, I threw my arms around her in a MASSIVE hug.

"You were BRILLIANT! I totally voted for you!" I squealed.

"Thanks," she said, hugging me back. "That means a lot, especially as WOLF BRETHREN were so good."

Another day I would have asked her if she was mental, but not today. "Yeah, they weren't bad." I hesitated and then rushed on before I lost my nerve. "Please can we stop fighting now and be friends? I've really missed you."

"I've missed you too," she replied, her eyes shining.

"Listen, I have to go and meet the twins. But I'll call you over the weekend. Oh, and Shen is here somewhere, if you want someone to share that WHAM BAR with."

She smiled and suddenly it was like the last six weeks had never happened. "Thanks, I will. Speak soon, Cass."

I left her and found Liam, deep in mutual congratulations with one of the REPERCUSSION team. I waited for him to spot me and stop talking. It didn't happen and I realized that our brief moment of being something like equals was over.

Well, almost over. "Hello? Auntie Jane will be here any minute," I said, interrupting the budding bromance. "Are you ready to go?"

Liam nodded. "Yeah, my HOMIES will sort all my stuff out. Let's blow this joint."

Now that he was no longer scared about Mum and the babies, his usual dorkiness was coming back. No one says homies any more. Shaking my head, I followed him out of the theatre but I couldn't hold down a feeling of excitement. My BFFs were mended, Nathan may or may not have just asked me out (squee!) and I was about to meet the twins for the very first time. Roll on Monday, I thought gleefully. Me, Molly and Shen had A LOT to talk about.

Reasons To
Be Cheerful

✳ Me, Shen and Molls are BFFs again – hurrah!

✳ Despite not being the brainiac everyone thought I
   was, I still turned out to be a bit of a quiz queen –
   bring on the national final in Oxford next term!

✳ The coolest boy in our year thinks I rock!
   And we are meeting up in the Christmas hols
   to plan our strategy for the nationals. Just the
   two of us – YAY!

✳ Discovered that Liam is not a moronic waste
   of space all of the time.

✳ I am finally a big sister!

✳ From a deeply unpromising start, my first term
   at St Jude's actually turned out to be made of win.
   It's not so bad being a muggle after all.

CHAPTER TWENTY

It took so long to get through the traffic that I was pretty sure the twins would be WALKING by the time we reached them. The hospital smelled of bleach and antiseptic but, given we were surrounded by newborn babies, it could have been a lot worse.

Mum was in her own little room, away from the hubbub of the ward. After her waters had broken, she and dad had rushed to the hospital and had got there with minutes to spare. He'd had to abandon the car outside the

labour ward and hurry inside with a heavily panting Mum.
The midwives had just got her onto a bed when the first
twin, JOSHUA, had arrived. His sister, ELSIE, had
appeared a few minutes later.

"I didn't even have time for any drugs," Mum said,
wincing at the memory. "Although your dad had a bit of
the gas and air."

Huh, that sounded about right, I thought as Dad stayed
completely unembarrassed. I bet the midwives had loved
him. I only hoped he hadn't broken out into Elvis, the way
he had when both me and Liam had been born. And I really
hoped he hadn't plumped for "RETURN TO SENDER".

The twins were even more SCRUMPTIOUS than I'd
imagined they'd be. Gazing at my brother and sister with
their tiny squashed-up faces, lying nose to nose under the
funny little knitted hats the nurse had given them, I felt
a sudden rush of love for my family. Now that the twins

were here, it felt like we were somehow complete and I was determined to be the best big sister ever. Of course, they'd have the worst big brother to put up with, too, but there wasn't much I could do about that. And he might not be so bad anyway; judging from the SOPPY look on his face, he was just as besotted with them as me.

I looked up at Mum and Dad, clearly exhausted but radiating happiness and felt a PDA coming on. Don't tell anyone I said this but maybe – just maybe – I'm glad I'm not adopted after all.

The End